STARS
THAT TURN

DAVID
NEWHOUSE

ISBN: 1461187540
ISBN 13: 9781461187547

To my at-home editors:

My family - Anne, Sam, and George;
The Anzicks;
All of my Language Arts classes over the years;
And my writer friends, Eric Pederson and
Alanna Cohen,
who nudged me over to the other side in the
first place.

CONTENTS

CHAPTER 1

WORDS

It was snowing slightly. Cathyn had her brown hood pulled up over her head as she waited by the well. From time to time she would look down into its dark depths. Her breath came out in little clouds of water vapor and washed over both sides of her face.

The well was next to a house that had fallen apart many seasons ago, once used by some early settlers in Normaneys, the small village that Cathyn called home. She knew why they had chosen such a spot—high up here on Ninian Ridge; they could have seen for miles down into the actual town and out across the valley to the Casandin Mountains.

This morning, just as yesterday, she had looked once again into the water in the well. At first her face was lost in shadow. But then her eyes focused, and she saw a girl of seventeen looking back up at her. This girl had long black hair spiraling out of the sides of her hood, falling in rivulets onto her cloak. Her skin was very fair, almost white. Her eyes, even at this distance, radiated a brilliant green. This girl, who Cathyn thought she knew, seemed completely and utterly lost. The face was open, as if it were the face itself that asked the question.

But this time when she looked down into the water, she saw it—slightly obscured by the reflection of the white clouds in the sky behind the image of her face and the mild ripples made by her own movements—a word.

Three days ago she had come up here to this well, scratched her name on a stone with her knife, and dropped it in. It was the only way to physically get in touch with Zia, the sorceress in the village, and she desperately needed her help. She knew that the response would take at least three days, but still she came up to the top of the ridge every day and looked down into the well. And now here it was at last, a word.

Cathyn squinted and leaned closer into the well so that the sides of her face were flanked by shadow. Her movement on the stones and her heavy breathing sent the water into a swell that washed away her own image. But the word remained, riding the tiny waves like a piece of white ribbon lost in the ocean. Was it just one word? What did it say? She remained as still as possible until the water settled.

Come.

Cathyn showed up on Zia's doorstep that same day. The sun was just starting to set, placing shadows in and around the house at odd angles. The snow was falling harder now.

Zia's house was little more than a cottage. Made of wood and stone and mud with a thick thatched roof, a chimney, and a rough porch on the front, it served as the main meeting place for the most important village concerns. Many of the farmers and merchants, wives and husbands, would come to Zia with questions or concerns about the weather, their crops, pregnancies, whatever they thought the witch could help them with.

She knocked on the old wooden door three times, pausing for a few moments in between, but there was no answer. A red-tailed hawk, secured to a perch with a multi colored rope, looked at her out of its sideways eyes. It opened its beak to make a sound, but remained mute. She tried the thin metal doorknob. It turned. She paused and opened it.

The room she entered was dark, but cozy. A small iron stove stood, legs spread wide, on a metal plate in the center of the wooden floor. Cathyn could see logs deep in its belly glowing brightly. It was the only light in the room, but it gave off a warmth that made Cathyn shiver. She pushed back her hood. A chair and a couch were next to the stove.

"Zia?" she called out as she unwound her scarf. There was no echo; the tightly packed house seemed to absorb sound. She closed the door behind her. "Zia?" she called again. "It's Cathyn. Cathyn Bood."

She could hear that her voice had caused something to move in the next room. She walked through the first room and into the second.

This room was as dark as the first. A large cage was on the floor; a monkey paced back and forth inside of it. It looked at Cathyn as she knelt down next to it.

"I have valuable information," the monkey whispered, looking around from side to side as if it had some deep, dark secrets to share.

Cathyn gasped and pulled back. She now saw that the monkey was actually more like a little man with a tail. Its teeth were sharp. It was covered in fur, but its face was very humanlike. It looked at her now with sad eyes, its tiny fingers wrapped around the bars.

"It tells you that so you'll let it out," came a voice behind her.

Turning around, Cathyn saw a woman. She was tall and lean with short black hair that swept partly over one eye, slight wings of hair arching on either side of the back of her collar. Her eyes were very dark, her face hard but handsome. She wore a long green skirt with detailed red-and-yellow runes embroidered in lines down the front and back. Her blouse was a simple white cotton. Over top of the blouse, she wore a short, open coat that matched her skirt. This was Zia, the sorceress.

Cathyn could not easily tell how old the witch was. She knew that her village neighbors had spoken of Zia for decades. All this time, Cathyn had imagined her as an old woman. Now she found herself guessing the woman's age as anywhere between thirty and fifty years old.

"Will you help me?" the creature pleaded.

Cathyn turned to the cage and back again to the sorceress. "How can you keep this creature locked up like this?"

Zia walked closer to Cathyn. She leaned over to a wall behind the cage and grabbed a walking stick. "If you want my help, I'll ask you to not judge my actions," she stated matter-of-factly. "Do you know what this thing is?"

Cathyn shook her head.

"It's an ittik. They're small, cute, and human-looking. They can even mimic speech. But they're also strong and extremely deadly. They'll gouge out your eyes just as soon as they look at you, and then steal everything you own."

The sorceress crouched down in front of the cage, next to Cathyn. She raised the stick and placed it just inside.

In an instant the end of the stick was snapped off. Cathyn could see a fury develop in the ittik's eyes as it threw the stick back toward them. The stick bounced off the inside of the cage, causing the creature to run back and forth and grab on to the bars. The cage was rocking, the ittik making a horrible screeching sound.

Zia stood up and motioned Cathyn to follow her. "Lovely manners, eh?" she asked as they left the room.

They walked through two other rooms. These rooms faced the setting sun and allowed in more light than the previous rooms. Cathyn noticed a gigantic thick oak table in one of the rooms, covered in papers, books, intricately designed boxes, and candles. In the other room, plants of all shapes, colors, textures, and sizes adorned the walls. A bowl on the floor emitted a yellow smoke that blanketed the room in a fine mist. Each room seemed to entertain a certain theme. It was strange, but Cathyn did not think that all of these rooms could be contained in the small house that she had seen outside. They talked as they walked.

"You need my help?" the witch asked, not looking at her.

"I do, Zia."

"Help costs something. How will you pay?"

"I was thinking," Cathyn said in a small voice, "that I could work for you."

"Work for me? What kind of work could a girl do for me?"

Cathyn was incensed. Her small voice disappeared. "I'm not just a girl! I am a warrior!"

The sorceress turned around. They were in a room that looked like a library. "You're not a warrior yet. But soon. I know who you are. And, more importantly, I know who your mother is."

The sorceress sat down in an old chair and motioned for Cathyn to do the same. A fire flared up in a nearby fireplace, taking Cathyn by surprise.

"You are Cathyn Bood, warrior daughter to Kaal Bood, the great archer and commander of the Second Color Militia. You've been attending the Academy since the age of…" She squinted at Cathyn.

"Seven," Cathyn finished for her.

Zia sighed. "Seven. And what are you now, fifteen?"

"Seventeen."

"One of your mother's arrows," Zia said.

"I beg your pardon?"

The sorceress looked at her hands. "You said you'd pay something for my advice. I want one of your mother's arrows."

"But why?" Cathyn realized it was an inappropriate question the moment she asked it.

Zia looked back at Cathyn. "That is for me to worry about and for you to do as I asked," she answered slowly, almost in a whisper.

The witch closed her eyes. She seemed to Cathyn as though she was initiating a meditation. "Your mother vanished almost six months ago. She has been believed dead all this time. But…" Here she opened her eyes and looked at the floor. "You do not think so." She smiled.

"You said 'is,'" whispered Cathyn.

The sorceress looked at Cathyn, eyebrows arched, a question on her face.

"You said 'is,' not 'was,' continued Cathyn. You said you know who my mother is." Cathyn swallowed. "You didn't say...you know...who my mother 'was.'"

The witch tilted her head as if trying to remember. "Did I?"

Cathyn looked closely at the woman. "You know something."

"Wise girl. You are your mother's daughter. But..." The witch stared hard into Cathyn's eyes. "You know something as well. Tell me what has sent you to me."

Cathyn hesitated, sat back in her chair, and breathed out. "I...had a vision a week ago."

Zia leaned forward. "You had a vision? What is this world coming to when warriors' daughters have visions?"

Cathyn remained straight-faced. "I saw my mother through my window. Not on the other side of my window, but actually within the window, like she was... caught...in the glass. I heard her speak to me. There was a rushing sound that made it hard for me to hear her words. It sounded like she was lost in a strong wind, but I did hear her say for me to come to her, that there would be someone sent soon to take me to her."

The ageless sorceress did not take her eyes from Cathyn. "She said that there would be someone sent for you? Did she tell you who this someone would be?"

Cathyn shook her head. "The vision died away after that. It just faded as if a shadow had wrapped it up in a bundle."

"Do you believe this vision to be true?"

"I do, Zia."

The witch was quiet for a long moment. "You have been trained for many years in the Academy. Does this not sound to you like a trap, someone sent to you to take you to her? Does this not sound...too easy?"

"All of these thoughts I have considered, Zia." Cathyn dropped her head. "I have tried to ignore it, but I cannot. My body begs me to go with this person, to see if my mother is alive or dead. That's why I've come to you...for guidance."

Zia looked at her hands again, thinking. She leaned back into the chair, crossed her legs. "What I tell you does not matter. You will do as you will." She gave a heavy sigh. "My advice is to ignore this vision. My sense is...that this is indeed a trap. You cannot go. Whatever it is that captured your mother, delayed her, is after you now. Because, child"—and here she looked right through Cathyn, at the empty space just past her—"there are things in this world, and in other worlds, of which you have no claim, things that thrive on the lives of those who live well, thrive on the souls of vibrant people. These soulless things hunt and prey on living, loving beings. Often it is enough to merely remain alive and not tempt this darkness that I speak of. One way to fight this darkness...is to live."

Cathyn did not move. She sat looking into Zia's dark eyes, transfixed, frightened. It seemed to Cathyn that, for just a moment, Zia's outline blurred and then recombined, as if she were transforming or fighting back a change in her physical being. Cathyn blinked and shook her head.

"But"—the sorceress moved back into her chair—"you will go. You will take your mother's weapons. You will follow this person into the dark. And perhaps you will find your mother. I know it is something that you will do."

Cathyn found her voice. "Yes...thank you...thank you, Zia," she whispered.

"You didn't need my advice at all, did you, girl?"

"Maybe not your advice. But your words."

The woman's face became serious, sharp as granite. "Words are just the air that dances on our skins. Words are the particles of light that surround us that we cannot touch. Words are the ripples of water leading back to the earth. Words are nothing to you now. Take your weapons."

CHAPTER 2
NINE NIGHTS

Cathyn's mother's "prophecy" had not mentioned when her mysterious guide would show up, only that he or she eventually would. So, like she had done for eight nights previously, Cathyn packed everything on the ninth night that she would need for the journey ahead: bread, dried meat, cheese, some dried fruit, two small flat flint stones, a pot, some spices, two cups, and her weapons—a knife that she would keep in a sheath strapped to her shin, a double-edged long-sword and its side scabbard, and her mother's battle recurve bow and marked arrows.

It was customary for warriors to make their own arrows. Each warrior had a distinctive color and mark that distinguished his or her weapons from another's. The arrows that Cathyn had packed into a deer hide side shoulder bag were an emerald green with three red dots placed in a line near the tip. The three fletchings, or guide feathers, were also a bright red. These arrows had been handcrafted by Cathyn's mother just before she had disappeared.

She remembered watching her mother making them in the work shed next to the house. It had been a cool, overcast spring morning, and she had noticed that her mother seemed distracted and somber as she lined up the long strips of wood in the foot-pump lathe.

Cathyn had mixed feelings about the arrows now; on the one hand, she couldn't stand the idea of losing them—they were as much a part of her mother as any fleeting memory that Cathyn still held on to. On the other hand, Cathyn was, like her mother, a warrior. She knew that she would use them when the time came. She knew that she would nock each arrow and release it in a rapid-fire blur without hesitation or even a second thought when it became necessary. But still, if she could manage to hold on to just one...

It was a small but resourceful estate on which she and her mother lived. The house was a well-sized one-story wood-and-stone structure with five rooms and a detached kitchen area. Two chimneys on either side of the house kept them warm in the winter. The solid foundation of the stone kept them cool when the temperatures turned hot.

There was a dark red barn sitting to the right of the house, which accommodated the three horses that they rode and cared for. One of these horses, a silver bay, belonged to her mother. He was predominantly a deep earth brown with a white mane and tail. Another horse was a buckskin with a cream-colored body and black mane, tail, and legs. Both animals were war-horses, raised and prepared to fight in battle. The third horse, Tempest, was Cathyn's horse, a beautiful salt-and-pepper with silver hairs entwined in the black that was most of his body. There were white patches around both of his eyes, giving the impression that the horse wore a mask. Cathyn loved this horse and believed that they shared a common telepathy. She often felt a kind of freedom when she rode Tempest that allowed her to almost become half human, half horse. Indeed, the horse would often turn before Cathyn knew where the next turn was coming.

The young warrior made it a priority to walk the horses each day (she actually rode Tempest every other day), leave them brushed, patted down, watered, and fed just in case she had to leave at a moment's notice. She had contacted a neighbor, Old Man Welsh, to check on the horses in a few days' time just in case she had gone. He was good with animals, horses in particular. He would know what to do if any trouble arose.

Another building to the left of the main house was a workroom that her mother and some of her fellow warriors had built to serve as a weapons room. Many of the weapons that Cathyn and Kaal Bood, as well as many of the warriors in the Second Color Militia, used were made here in this building. Along with a supply of wood, leather, iron, and charcoal, it also housed a forge.

The rest of the estate was comprised of some field areas (one section used for a self-sustaining garden) and then a mass of thick woods that spread out to become the larger Mammoth Woods.

And so, for eight nights she had packed her riding satchel, oiled and polished her longsword, oiled the leather hilt attached to it, and restrung and waxed her bow. She would then wake early, walk the width and breadth of her and her mother's estate, attend to the horses and a few chores around the house, and wait. When late noon finally came and nothing happened, she would unpack everything, unstring her bow, and curse this absent guide. And now, here, on the ninth night, she did it one more time.

Cathyn awoke this morning with no extra sense of foreboding. The snow had stopped many days ago, but the air was still cold and crisp. Layers of white decorated the trees and bushes about their house.

She went to the kitchen to fix a small breakfast of buttered toast, some sliced pears from her and her mother's supply of canned fruit, and tea and took it to the front porch. She set it down on a small table and went back into the house to fetch her longsword, which she put on the floor next to her chair.

When she looked up, she saw a man standing straight as a board, fifty yards from the front of her house, hands clasped behind his back, looking directly at her. A pure white stallion stood behind him, not far off, tied to a small tree. It looked feral, wild. Although it had been blanketed and saddled to make riding more comfortable for the rider and the horse, its mane and coat were long and unkempt; its hooves were unshod.

The yard all about her was silent. Odd. Not even the chatter of the winter birds that would often wake her on late mornings.

She picked up her sword and walked toward the man. He did not move, only watched her intently. Although Cathyn's sword-in-hand approach could be regarded as threatening, the man remained still. He looked like a statue. Cathyn noticed, through the hovering mist that left her own mouth as she walked, that no breath seemed to escape from this man's mouth.

His skin was marble white. He sported a full black mustache, but aside from that, was clean-shaven, even bald. He wore a gray coat buttoned up to the collar, gray pants, and tall black boots. His gray pants were tucked inside the boots. A sword was sheathed on his left side. It looked as long as Cathyn's, but it sported a golden and ornate pommel at the end of a white bone grip. A fancy cross guard sprouted between the hilt and the locket on the scabbard.

As Cathyn got closer, she noticed a patch on the man's coat, just over the heart. It was a design that she had never seen before—two black swords side by side at an angle in the middle of a red triangle. The black swords hovered within the left and right sides. At the top of the triangle was a glowing sun.

"You are who the...vision said would come to guide me to my mother?" Cathyn asked.

"I am," the gray man replied, still barely moving.

"No doubt you know who I am," Cathyn continued.

"No doubt."

"Then who are you?"

"My name is Captain Melog."

"What army are you with, Melog? I do not recall that insignia from any of the local armies near here," Cathyn said, pointing to the patch on his coat.

"Certainly not local, dear heart. It is an army that, I dare say, you would not be aware of, an army...far from here," Melog answered, uncrossing his black-gloved hands from behind his back and bringing them down loosely to his sides. He tipped his head slightly and smiled, looking down at her.

"Whom do you serve?" Cathyn asked.

Melog's smile vanished. "I serve only one. That is all you need to know for now."

"And who is this 'one' whom you serve?"

The gray man just looked at her. There was no attempt to answer this question anywhere on his face.

Cathyn took a deep breath. "How long will this journey take, Captain?"

"One day, one night, and part of another day," he replied. "There is a special path that we must take that will bring us to the other side."

"The other side?"

"It's...where your mother is."

The horse made a sound behind him, and Melog turned slightly. The horse obviously did not like being tied up. Cathyn guessed that the gray man was ascertaining whether the horse would hold steady.

Melog turned back and brought his hands up to his chest. His gloves were as black as his boots. One hand loosely massaged the other as if the glove was too tight. He looked up at the sky and squinted, his manner remaining serious. "We should leave as soon as possible," he commented. "Are you ready?"

Cathyn paused for a moment. "One more question, Captain. What proof do you have that my mother is still alive?"

Captain Melog reached into his right coat pocket and pulled out an armband. He dropped it into Cathyn's hand. It was her mother's armband, marked with the same colors and markings as the arrows that lay in the shoulder bag in her house. It was the armband that Kaal Bood wore when she went into battle.

"This is hardly proof that my mother is alive," Cathyn whispered.

"It's the best I can do," Melog replied.

Cathyn said nothing, but turned and walked back to the house.

When she returned, she was riding Tempest. She had her backpack and weapons and was stuffing the last of her breakfast into her mouth. She had on high brown riding boots with her knife sheathed closely to her leg, just inside her right boot. Her pants and three layers of shirts were shades of browns and greens. She wore her thick brown cloak with the hood pulled up. Underneath her cloak, and unbeknownst to Captain Melog, she proudly wore her mother's battle armband. Her longsword was in its scabbard sturdily buckled to her belt and dangling down the horse's left side. Her mother's bow was wrapped across her chest and left shoulder, the arrows in a quiver on her back.

She trotted up to Captain Melog, who was already mounted on his horse. When she looked closer at the horse, she noticed that it had red eyes and a strange mark on its forehead, a red blemish that resembled a sun that had burned out. The horse had a wild look in its feral eyes, but also an intelligence that she had never seen in an animal like this before.

They were quite a pair, these two riders, a portrait of opposites—Cathyn, all browns and greens, riding on her salt-and-pepper, and Captain Melog, all grays and blacks, riding on his pure white.

"I'm ready, Melog. Lead on," she said, still chewing.

The gray man looked at her with interest. "You don't seem too worried about all of this," he remarked.

"I've suspected all along that this could be a trap, Captain. But I go into it with eyes wide open. If this is the only way that I can reunite with my mother, then so be it. But be forewarned; I regard you as an enemy."

"And a guide," Melog added.

"Yes, and a guide. It's a problematic relationship at best. But I can walk that fine line if need be."

"Wise girl," Melog said as he turned toward the mountains. "Just like your mother."

Where had she heard that before?

CHAPTER 3
BARK

They trotted at a leisurely pace through the little village that Cathyn had called home her entire life. She had never lived anywhere else. From time to time, she would see villagers whom she recognized. No one questioned where she was going or the mysterious man on the strange horse who accompanied her. They seemed to know that it was an important journey, something tied to Cathyn's missing mother. Although they did give Captain Melog the odd stare. Was Cathyn in any trouble? Was she riding on her own power, or held captive by this gray rider? She assuaged their unspoken fears by returning their nods and their waving hands with a smile and a wink.

Eventually, their riding brought them to the north edge of the town where Zia lived. Cathyn could see smoke curling from the chimney of Zia's house. It made her want to stop and tell the witch good-bye, maybe get one last bit of advice before she left, or a magical assessment of the gray man who rode with her. But she knew that Captain Melog would not permit it. He seemed determined and time-bent.

Regardless, she pulled up to Zia's yard and dismounted. She knew that Tempest would stay where she left him; he was still in familiar territory. As she walked up to the witch's front porch, she pulled one of her mother's arrows from her quiver and put it on a small table. Zia's request. Cathyn looked at the lone arrow for a few moments and then mounted Tempest. She rode up to join Captain Melog.

She wondered if Zia was watching them from one of her windows as they passed by. The last thing that Cathyn saw of her village home was the perch outside Zia's house that had once held her red-tailed hawk. The hawk was not there.

The sun had ticked ahead three or four positions in the sky. They had, by now, left Normaneys far behind and were well on their way toward the Casandin Mountains. Cathyn and her mother had ridden to those mountains many times, had dismounted their horses and spent the day and a night hunting there together. These mountains were not alien to her now. They were, in fact, a return. The Academy lay 100 kilometers to the south, a long carriage ride over main roads and through ever-growing villages. Cathyn had been back and forth that way many times. But, truth be told, she had never ridden up, over, and past these mountains in her lifetime. And she knew that she would ride past them today.

Once they were off the main road now packed in new snow, they took a turn to the left and began to cut their way through the farthest edge of Mammoth Woods. Staying on man-made walking and riding paths that had been forged by hikers and woodsmen and traders years ago, and then reforged again by more recent visitors to the forest, the two riders wound their way through the leafless winter treescape.

A movement just out of the edge of Cathyn's vision warned her that they were not alone. She shot a quick glance up ahead at Captain Melog, who did not seem to see what she did. She turned all the way around in her saddle to get a more complete view of the winter forest, but there was no sign of anyone else nearby. Tempest even seemed concerned. The horse turned his head sideways from time to time in an effort to catch Cathyn's eyes. His breathing became labored. He seemed as anxious as Cathyn had just become.

Then it happened again. Strange. A movement, but no sound to accompany it. Another blur to her left. Melog had seen it that time. He slowed his horse down to a halt. He sat and listened. No sound, save for the cracking of various branches as they succumbed to the weight of the recent ice and snow.

And then it came to her—Bark. Cathyn and her mother had come across him many times, but not always, when they rode this way. The old story was that a woodcutter had gone into the forest after the death of his wife to cut down a tree and bring back the wood for her casket, but he had suddenly gone mad and decided to stay. He became a hermit, and the children in Normaneys had named him Bark. No one could even remember his true name. He had decided to call the woods his home. He was not considered dangerous. He moved about, not staying in one place, sleeping in caves or trees or sometimes, when the weather got particularly bad, in makeshift shelters that he constructed out of the plentiful wood that now surrounded him. He was also, apparently, silent as a shadow as he moved between the trees.

When Cathyn turned her head back toward the snow-covered path, Bark was standing before them, blocking their way. Not saying anything. Just standing. It startled Tempest, and he backed up. Cathyn patted his neck and whispered to him reassuringly.

The old hermit of the forest was dressed in many layers of deerskin and fur, with boots and large mitten gloves made of cloth, and a funny fur hat with two tiny antlers coming out of it. He had a very long white beard caked with frost and ice. His hair was also long and white, and it lay across his shoulders and down his back. He was missing the tip of his nose, probably due to frostbite. Cathyn could not tell how old he was. She had heard his story for years, ever since she was old enough to be told such things by her mother, late at night, as they sat around the hearth sewing or cleaning weapons. But he looked now as old as time.

"The young woman goes somewhere?" he said. He was almost smiling. The cold of the forest did not seem to affect him in the least.

"Get out of our way," Captain Melog hissed.

"I talk to her." Bark pointed at Cathyn.

"And I talk to you." The guide did not back down.

Cathyn spoke up. "Melog, it's all right." She turned back to the forest man. "This is Bark. My mother and I have seen him many times in this forest. Isn't that right, Bark?"

The old man began to bark like a dog. It made the horses uneasy. "Bark," he said. "Is it because I bark?"

"It's because the trees are protected by bark as you are now protected by the trees," Cathyn anwered.

This made Bark smile. "Yes. Good answer, young woman," he said. "Where to on this fine winter's day?"

Cathyn thought about this. How much to tell him? "We're...going to see my mother, Bark. She's been missing for many months now."

This made Bark's smile fade. "Oh...I know that. I remember that." He pointed at Cathyn. "The young woman's momma was taken. I saw that. Not fair. Not fair, the way she was taken. I think that you ride in danger." The old woodcutter gave Melog a rough stare.

"What did you see, Bark?" Cathyn asked, now curious. Could he have seen what happened? Was it here in the woods? She shifted in her saddle.

He ignored the question. "The trees talk to me, even in the winter. They are old. They are cold. But they talk to me still. They know things. Do you know how they know things?" He got down on all fours and put his ear to the ground near the roots of a tall, hibernating oak. "They are connected to the ground and all the things that run inside the ground." He stood back up, snow now on the side of his face. He did not bother to wipe it off. Cathyn could see that he was missing his ear. Only a bruised and purple hole was left. "The young woman's momma was not taken by accident." He looked up at Cathyn. "Surely the young woman knows this?" There was a beseeching look on his face.

"Enough of this," warned Captain Melog. "This man is mad. He delays us." He turned back to Bark. "Get out of the way, or I will ride over you."

Cathyn ignored him. "What kind of danger, Bark?"

Bark turned his head from side to side, a sudden wild look in his eyes. "Do you hear that?" He turned again. "She grabs you tight, and she holds on for dear life!" he wailed. He scrunched his face up and hugged his arms around himself.

"Who, Bark? My mother?"

"There!" He pointed behind them. He screamed.

They swiveled suddenly in their saddles to look. Melog pulled his sword, prepared for unforeseen danger, but the path behind them was empty. When they turned back, Bark was gone. They had not heard him leave.

The riders were silent for more than a few heartbeats as Cathyn took in everything that the hermit had said.

"Do not take anything into account about what that wild man ranted," stated Captain Melog as he resheathed his sword. "He knows nothing of what he speaks. He's mad. He's just trying to scare you so he can have the woods all to himself."

"Maybe," Cathyn remarked. "But there is something in his madness that I think speaks of a universal truth."

"Bah," was all Melog would comment.

"He seemed so sincere," Cathyn said to herself. "And I think he does hear the trees. In a strange way, I think the trees do talk to him." She turned in her saddle and regarded the quiet winter forest again in a whole new way, as if a curtain had been drawn aside.

CHAPTER 4

KING OF THE AIR

By late in the afternoon, Cathyn realized that she no longer recognized any of this part of Mammoth Woods that Captain Melog had recently been guiding her through. She thought that she had been here before, knew that she had climbed the Casandin Mountains, now looming before them, many times with her mother. But now it was all so unfamiliar. Had it been that long ago since they had left the comfort of her and her mother's house? No, merely the change from early morning to now. She should still be able to pick out something that she had seen before-a path, a rock, a tableau of small trees. But nothing looked the same. She noticed that the temperature was changing as well; it was getting warmer. They had left the fresh snow behind. It was now almost like fall, and getting warmer by the moment. The snow that had crunched beneath their horses' hooves earlier was now beginning to transition into patches of dirt and rocks. Time seemed to be going backward even as they pressed on forward.

And Captain Melog—the way he rode just ahead of her, never seeming to tire, eyes always forward, no conversation unless Cathyn instigated it—he was a strange man. In her stomach, Cathyn did not trust him. He was far too gracious, too condescending.

"Captain Melog!" Cathyn half shouted. "When are we going to come to that path that you were talking about?"

Melog did not look back. "We are on the path, dear heart. Didn't you know?"

Cathyn had suspected that the change had already taken place. But it was a way to get some of her questions answered, or at the very least, a way to get some kind of affirmation for what she suspected was happening. Indeed, it seemed as though they had crossed over to another entire world.

"You were expecting something else?" he asked. "A shimmering rainbow, perhaps? A doorway? An explosion of light? I'm sorry if I've disappointed you. No. Paths such as this one are oftentimes right under our noses." He touched his own nose as if to illustrate the idiom. "All the time. All around us if we just know how to get to them. And then how to use them to our best advantage."

Condescending. Were all her questions to be turned into cat-and-mouse games? "You said this journey would take two days and one night?"

"I should think so," Melog answered. "Unless unforeseen…things get in the way."

"Unforeseen things? Like what?"

Melog paused. Was he thinking about how to answer her, or just upset that he had to answer her?

"Oh, I don't know, dear heart," he sighed. "These particular woods can be very surprising. One can walk along for days and not come across anything unusual. And then…well, there's no telling what kind of… obstacle may get in your way."

Their pathway through the forest began to rise upward into the mountain. The riders leaned forward on their steeds, bouncing with them and urging them on over boulders and around bushes and turns in the earth. It was a gentle climb up the mountains, but a long one. Cathyn was glad she was on Tempest. Doing this by foot would have taken too long, would have worn her out. The horses were both good climbers. The ascent was uneventful, save for an occasional snake that threatened to startle the horses, or a deer that peered out at them between the high boulders.

"Does your horse have a name?" Cathyn asked suddenly.

Her guide did not answer right away. Had he heard her, or was he just being rude?

"No name," finally came the reply.

"Your horse is named Noname?"

Melog paused again. "It does not have a name. It is just a horse."

No sense of humor. "Oh. My horse's name is Tempest," Cathyn pressed on.

"Good to know."

This was going to be a longer journey than Cathyn had originally thought.

Presently they crested the first peak of the mountain range. Cathyn noticed some berries grouped about a bush and decided to stop and pick them. She dismounted Tempest and took off her cloak, now too warm in the changing season. She removed one of her layers of shirts and stuffed it and the cloak into her pack. Captain Melog saw her and stopped. He turned his horse, but did not dismount.

When Cathyn got closer to the berries, she realized that they looked like berries she had eaten before. They were the same color, but these were smaller, and they had a shine to them that the others did not. She remembered when her mother had introduced them to her. They had been on a hunting expedition. Her mother had brought along goat's milk, and they had heated the milk and poured it over the berries. The berries had burst open, releasing a sweet juice that mixed in the warm milk. It was delicious. Cathyn's mouth watered just looking at them. She bit just a part of one and decided that they were not poisonous. They were very much like the berries her mother had shown her. More delicious, even.

"Captain Melog, I'm resting here for a bit. Care for something to eat?"

The gray man looked over her head at the trees and the unclouded sky. "Rest? Yes, we can rest for a while," he said. He slid down from his horse in one fluid motion. He pulled out some oats from his pack and held out his hand for the horse to eat. "But not for long, dear heart. We are on a tight schedule."

Cathyn found a spot next to a small boulder and opened up the backpack on her saddle. She pulled out a wrapped cloth and put it in her pocket. She took this time to feed Tempest. When her horse had finished eating, Melog grabbed both of them by the reins and led them over to a small spring that was running nearby.

Cathyn opened up the cloth and took out a packet of meat that had been wrapped in dried leaves. She tore off a small piece. "I don't like not knowing where I'm going, Captain Melog!" she yelled over to him. "This is one step away from kidnapping."

Captain Melog turned his head from the horses. "It's not my job to answer your questions." He squinted at Cathyn as she sat on the ground, her back against a boulder. "I will tell you this, though…" He looked up at the sky between the trees. "We need to get past Abathet Woods before nightfall."

Cathyn unhooked her mother's bow from around her neck and shoulders. She put it on the ground next to her. "Abathet Woods? Never heard of them," Cathyn muttered between bites.

"I'll grant there's much here you've never heard of," Melog answered. "They're just at the top of this last summit."

An ominous note. Was he trying to scare her? He'd have to try harder than that. Cathyn had been raised on stories of great battles and death and perilous rescues and monsters. She had come to believe that she herself would be a part of such a violent history some day. It was a duty that was expected in a warrior family.

She stabbed another piece of meat with her knife and offered it to her guide.

Melog shook his bald head. "I don't eat," he said as he walked back to where she sat. The horses remained tied to a tree next to the spring where they continued drinking.

"You don't eat?" Cathyn asked.

"I don't eat."

There was more silence between them. The man was becoming stranger and stranger to her with every passing moment. Was he made of magic? Was he a sorcerer too, like Zia? Or was he something else?

Suddenly there was a wild rustling in the air. Cathyn's mind and body went into warrior mode. Wings flapping, coming in close. Something large.

In an instant she had leaped up and grabbed her knife from her shin sheath. As soon as the thing came into her field of vision, all browns and reds and a blur of movement too close to see clearly, she drove her knife forward toward its belly. A hand caught her knife hand so fast that all of her muscles locked. She got her first glimpse of the thing.

It was almost as large as she was, with a wingspan twice her height. Its wings, not feathers, but membranes, beat the air about them as it tried to keep its balance and hold on to her at the same time. It was like wrestling two creatures, or three. Cathyn could see its bony hand shaking the knife in her grip, its fingers long and calloused, ridged along the knuckles, its skin more like stone than flesh. She could tell from the powerful grip that this creature's bones were light for flying, but extremely strong.

Cathyn dropped the knife. Captain Melog was swinging his sword at the creature's back. It made impact, but seemed to have little effect. It clanged as it bounced off its spine. Another winged creature took hold of the guide from behind and easily lifted him up into the air. The creature grabbed his sword in midair with its clawlike foot and dropped the weapon to the ground. They both disappeared out of sight.

The thing's grip on Cathyn was bone-crushing. It pulled her along the dust and dirt in zigzags, now and then stopping just long enough to bang her head into the ground. She grunted, but did not let go. It flew-jumped on top of her, pinning her down on her back, its face close to her own face. She pushed up hard on its shoulders and pulled her head back just to get a better look.

It was the face of a dog, but different. The snout was smaller than a dog's, but the eyes were enormous, probably needed for hunting high in the air. It was twisting its neck furiously to get a bite out of her. She could only imagine what her face would look like after a bite from those teeth. If it made contact with her neck, she'd be finished. She used her forehead and struck the monster full-force in the mouth. She heard a clunk and a screech, and the thing released her, half flapping, half running to get some distance between them. Good. At least the fleshy parts of their faces were vulnerable.

Cathyn was on one knee rearming herself with her knife and ready for another attack. She felt a trickle of blood running down her face from her forehead.

The hound-thing was sitting on top of a boulder, crouched, looking at her. It was catching its breath. She could see its torso heaving back and forth. Another moment to catch her own breath, and she would charge.

"Who are you?" the creature yelled in between gulps. The volume of its voice was tremendous. It breathed some more, gasped at the air. "Who are you?" it yelled again.

Cathyn decided to take the offense. She used the back of her sleeve to wipe at the blood on her head. "Attack me again, and I'll put a hole in your wings!" she yelled. "Where is my guide?"

The creature looked up at the sky and made a sound. Was it a laugh? Cathyn felt sure that it was.

It moved its wings slowly, as if to taunt her, and pulled itself up to its full height. "You talk to king like that?" Its voice was still shouting. It didn't seem to have a speaking voice. Maybe that was the only voice it could have for communicating long distances in the air. "I am king of Air. You talk to king like that, then when you sleep, I take you in sky way up. You not see river or tree or mountain. I take you so far up, all you see is lines and circles, like drawings in sand. Then you cry. Then I let you go. You fall. Too bad. It take so long to fall, you die many time over. Then you see lines and circles come up fast in face. Blattt! All flat on ground. Dead. In many pieces. Even bone go flat. I call brothers and sisters in Air. We come over and eat you flesh and drink meat in bone. Nice meal. Thank you!"

All of this had come at Cathyn in rapid-fire order. And loud. The images raised the hairs on the back of her neck. But her mother had prepared her for many kinds of fights. She called its bluff and walked over to it, knife held straight out in front of her, pointing.

Still holding the knife, she bent quickly to pick up her mother's bow. Then she threw the knife in the dirt directly in front of the dog-bat-thing. It jumped and fluttered off the rock. She took the time to nock an arrow in the bowstring. She did this cooly and deliberately and aimed it at the creature's throat.

"Why did you attack me? Tell me, or your head is gone!"

The thing was transfixed, frozen to the boulder. Cathyn couldn't tell if it was getting ready to spring or if it was just thinking about what to say. "You have aura," it said. "I see aura from sky. It different color. You not from this side."

"I have an aura," Cathyn repeated. "You can see that?"

"Big eye, see many thing." It pointed at its eyes. "Aura tell me you cross over. Bad magic you be here."

"What kind of bad magic?" Cathyn bobbed the bow slightly, reminding the creature where it was pointing and what it could do.

"You stay too long, aura grow. Aura take over Air, space, tree. This side get sick. Die. I kill you first. You see?"

"I don't plan to stay here that long," Cathyn explained. "I'm here to find someone." She paused. "Once I find her, we'll leave. We won't come back."

The creature wasn't satisfied. "You with man with no blood?"

"Man with no blood? What are you talking about?"

"You with man with no blood." This time it was a statement. "I see. He bring you here to Other Side."

"His name is Captain Melog. He is my guide. And right now I'm missing him. You cannot kill him. I need him to help me find this person." She paused. "What do you mean he has no blood?"

"I see." It blinked. "No blood. No aura. No soul."

"What do you see if there's no aura?" Cathyn asked. Now she was interested. More information about this man who was leading her…where?

The bat-dog-thing reared its head and seemed to sigh. It looked back at Cathyn. "I see…black. Aura no there, it go inside. Light go in, get caught. Not come back out. Black. Black hole." It paused again. "Nothing."

Cathyn rolled this around in her head. What was it telling her about this guide whom she was entrusted to follow? "Will you let me finish my business in peace?" Cathyn asked.

"You go once you find who you look?"

"Yes."

"You not kill king of Air?"

"Yes, I will not kill you."

"Promise?" It almost smiled as it tilted its dog face and waved its finger at her.

"Promise."

The thing nodded. It raised its head back and cupped its hands to its mouth. A terrifying screech pierced the air. The second creature fluttered into view and let go of a struggling Captain Melog, who dropped to the ground, landing gently on his feet.

Cathyn heard a sound behind her, stones on the ground. As she turned, she heard the creature lift up into the air. In a blur, it was gone.

Captain Melog approached her, dusting himself off. He stooped to pick up his dropped sword. "What happened here?" he asked. "Are you all right?" He seemed genuinely concerned about her welfare. Whoever had sent him on this mission expected him to keep Cathyn alive and well.

Cathyn slacked the arrow in the bow, brought her arms down. "What were those things?" she asked.

"Gulunay," the guide answered. "They are fierce hunters. You fought it off." He seemed genuinely impressed. "The one that grabbed me should have killed me. I don't know why it did not. Perhaps to bargain with you. I think they were more interested in you than me."

"I did make a bargain with it," Cathyn confessed.

"What kind of bargain?"

"That we would go as soon as I found my mother."

Melog shrugged, cracked his neck. "And it agreed to this? How interesting."

"This is a strange world, Melog."

"Indeed," was all he said.

Cathyn clenched her jaw and shouldered her bow, picking up her knife and food cloth. All was silent except for the sound of small rocks rolling down a hill. Cathyn remained staring at Captain Melog until, without a word, he turned to get the horses.

CHAPTER 5
ABATHET WOODS

It was almost dusk now when a wall of trees stretched out across the mountain pass in front of them. Melog did not stop to take in the view as Cathyn did. They were near the top summit of what used to be the Casandin Mountains, though Cathyn knew they were somewhere else entirely. The two horses held their positions on the sloping and rocky earth.

"These are Abathet Woods?" asked Cathyn.

"They are," sighed Captain Melog without turning around. "These woods must be gotten through as quickly as possible, before nightfall."

"I've never seen such a thick forest so high in the mountains before."

Melog just looked at her. She knew what his answer would be, probably ending in the phrase "dear heart."

The trees grew over the entrance to the forest in a dark, thick arc. Their branches came together like they were holding hands, moving in a dance so slow, nothing human could see it.

Captain Melog stopped his horse right at the entrance. Looking up at the sun heading now toward the horizon, he squinted and turned to look back at the mountain that they had just climbed.

"What are we waiting for?" asked Cathyn.

He did not answer her, instead took out a small, polished sphere from one of his many pockets and held it close to his eye.

"What is that?" asked Cathyn again.

Again Melog did not answer, just continued thinking, looking around them, and then checking the mysterious sphere.

"Melog, you're infuriating when you do that."

"Do what?"

"When you don't talk to me."

"Oh," he sighed, looking at the sky through the small sphere. "In need of some conversation, are we?"

Cathyn lazily walked Tempest up next to Melog's white stallion. With lightning speed, she swiped at Melog's hand, grabbing the sphere from it as if by magic.

The guide looked at her, eyes half closed. His gaze hardened to a kind of focused intensity. The stallion moved backward slowly. Melog directed it forward again. He put out his opened hand. Cathyn paused, then dropped the sphere into it.

"Don't ever play with me like that again," he hissed. "You have no idea what you're dealing with." He turned his head back to the sky behind them. "I could crack you like an egg."

Cathyn breathed in slowly. She lowered her head slightly to swallow; she did not want him to see the movement in her neck. Cathyn harbored no doubts about what he could do to her. Warrior or no warrior, she was no match for this man. "I'd just like some answers sometimes." She looked down at his hand. "For instance, what is that...sphere?"

He looked back at her. "I don't believe it's my job to explain any of this to you."

"Then what is your job, Melog?"

His answer was slow and precise. "My job is to get you to where your mother is, and that is all." He looked back down at his hand. "Now, I'd advise you to leave me to it."

After a few moments, Melog pocketed the sphere and drew himself erect in the saddle. Without another word, he swung his horse back to the opening in the woods and slowly rode through the natural opening. Cathyn followed.

With the dark, colorless figure and his white horse ahead of her, Cathyn took in her surroundings. The trees on either side of her were so closely grown together, all she could make out were the branches and trunks and high-standing roots and vines. It all appeared to be one great mass of plant material. Could any animals live in here? It seemed, actually, too dense, too overgrown, too dark for animal life. And still, along with these observations, came the instincts of a warrior. This was not a safe place. Even Melog seemed anxious. She could feel her body tensing up for something...anything...the unexpected.

It wasn't a sound that alerted her. Indeed, there had been no sound at all, just a sixth sense that told Cathyn she was being watched, and that she must turn around now. And as she turned, she thought she saw a fire moving toward them from the trees. It seemed to be moving along with them. She was about to warn Melog of a fire when she noticed that it wasn't a fire at all, but a faint outline of something. And the outline was disturbing the air around it. It was like looking through the air above a fire, and the shimmering heat that emanates from it, making what you're looking at dance and sway as if underwater. The outline that was approaching her was almost invisible, but not quite. Even Tempest reacted to it, pawing the ground and backing away. It was behind Melog, so he did not see it.

All the while she was watching and turning and riding, she was also cocking her bow. Whatever was approaching them, it must be stopped. Without a word, she shot just ahead of the fleeting object in the precise direction that it was headed. Not bad for riding a moving horse. The arrow tore through the shimmering figure without any effect, sending the shaft deep into a tree behind it. The thing stopped its approach just long enough for Cathyn to unsheathe her longsword and realize that it was not just one figure, but three…all grouped together.

"Melog!" she called out and nodded in the direction of the thing.

The gray man had already looked over at the sound of her arrow piercing the tree. He turned his horse and cautiously drew his sword.

"You are as a phantom, and my arrows cut right through you!" Cathyn yelled, holding her sword in bent-arm position, blade at the ready. "But you won't take us easily, I can assure you! If there's anything on your transparent bodies that can be cut, we will cut it!"

Melog looked on. The thing was now walking slowly toward them both. The gray man repositioned his sword in his other black-gloved hand.

"Who are you?" demanded Cathyn.

One of the things made a noise that resembled speaking, but the language was indecipherable. It sounded like a series of crackles and static.

In one swift movement, Melog leaned down from his horse and cut a side swath through the transparent creature, with no effect. They could hear the low whoosh of the sword as it sliced at nothing. His stallion sidestepped away.

The phantom spoke again, a different voice this time, but still without making sense. It moved closer to Captain Melog. One of the figures reached out toward Melog's horse. The guide's sword sliced at what would have been a wrist. It made a crackling sound as it entered the thing's body, but, again, did not cut anything.

Then another of the figures grabbed Cathyn and made contact with her left leg, still in the stirrups. It was a strong grip. Cathyn looked at the thing that had grabbed her and was instantly aware that it was changing before her eyes. The transparency was filling in, replaced now with skin and hair and clothes. A crackling sound had started the moment the thing had touched her, coupled with the strange language that the thing was speaking, but now the sound had hummed away. An eerie vibration coursed through her body as if replacing her blood with pins and fire. It rattled her to the bones.

Standing before her and her horse, firmly gripped to her leg, was a large, barrel-chested man with bushy black hair and a bushy black beard. The crackling sound was now replaced with normal speech.

"So sorry, missy. We didn't mean to frightens you. It's just that this is the only way we's can do this," he said.

Tempest calmed down as soon as the human materialized. The horse seemed oddly comforted by the bushy-bearded man's presence.

Cathyn again tried to break the bond by lifting her leg out of the stirrups, but without success. "Do what? Who are you?" she half shouted.

By this time, two other of the ghostlike figures had taken hold of her right leg on the other side of her horse and were also materializing into fully formed men. One of the men on her right was tall and thin, bald, like Captain Melog, but clean-shaven and with a long, hooked nose. The third one was plump. He had long, straight hair parted down the middle and tied in a ponytail, a mustache, and goatee on his chin. His nose was large and bulbous, and his cheeks were pudgy. He beamed a huge smile at Cathyn when she looked at him. His eyes twinkled. He seemed honestly happy to see her.

The one with the bushy beard looked quickly at Captain Melog, who was approaching them now with raised sword. "Put down your sword, sir!" he warned. "We have your companion. If you wants her alive, sir, put down your sword."

The guide stopped in his tracks.

"Kettle's right there, your lordship," said the tall, skinny man eyeing Captain Melog. "Could you put away your sword there? It can cut us sure enough now, and I can't stands the sight of blood, leastways me own, if'n you knows what I mean?" He smiled.

"Tell 'em who we are, Kettle," said the plump one.

"You can let go of me now," whispered Cathyn between clenched teeth. The men's grips on her legs were incredibly strong. They had her virtually pinned to her own horse. She knew she could not break them.

"Well, you see, missy...there's the rub," continued the one with the bushy beard, the one the other two had called Kettle. "We really can't lets go. It's the only way we'll be able to makes any sense."

"Ahhh...it feels so good to be...solid again!" piped up the plump man. "Don't it, Gamliggy?"

"I knows whats you mean, Pitts," answered the skinny one. "I believes I can feel the wind on me cheeks! Is that the wind on me cheeks, Kettle?"

"Perhaps we'd all better just sit down on that rock over there for a bits." Kettle motioned with his chin. "Everyone just remain calm, and I'll explain everythin'."

The skinny one called Gamliggy cocked his head and made his eyes large for Cathyn. "You wouldn't happen to have the makings for a nice cup of tea now, would you, mum? We could help you fix it up. Is it in that saddle pack there?"

Kettle furrowed his brow and shook his head. "Not the time, Gamliggy," he whispered.

Cathyn's eyes narrowed. "My captain here cares not for my safety, I can assure you," Cathyn lied. "Either you release me this instant or he slices off all of your heads faster than you can say one lump or two."

"That's funny, ain't it, Kettle!" snorted the skinny one called Gamliggy. "One lump or two!"

"I don't thinks she was talkin' about the tea," whispered Pitts.

"She wasn't?" asked Gamliggy. "What were she talkin' about, then?"

"She were talkin' about our heads," clarified Pitts.

"Oh...then I don't get it."

"Stop it, the two of you!" Kettle barked from the other side of the horse. "Now, now, missy," he continued in a gentler tone, "there's no need to get all worked up like that. I'll tell you what...How's 'bout we release you with the promise that, once you gets yerself all settled down and comfortable like, we grab hold of yous again so's...we can talk about this?"

"I've got a better idea," offered Captain Melog, leaning down from his horse. "How about if I slice off all of your heads at the same time, watch them roll away, thus sparing us from hearing anything from you that we don't actually want to hear in the first place?" He had yelled the last eleven words at full volume.

There was a long pause. "Naw...I don't fancy that idea one bit...not one bit," said Gamliggy in a conversational tone. "Do you like that idea, Pitts?"

"Can't say as I do, Gamliggy. How about you, Kettle? You like his lordship's idea?"

Kettle sighed and turned back to Cathyn. "The fact is, missy, we need your help. We desperately need your help. If'n yous kills us now, you'd just be killin' three innocent men what don't means you no harm. I don't thinks we have a thing to offer the two of yous, but we could use your help desperately. So, what do you say, missy? If'n we lets you go, and we gives yous a chance to get a nice fire goin'..."—here he looked at Gamliggy's legs, which he could see from his side of the horse—"and a bit of water on the boil for tea, then...cans we hold on to yous again later...for just a bit? That's when we'll be explainin' our predicament. It makes for a good story, and everybody likes to hear a good story now and again, don't you think?"

Cathyn looked at Melog. He gave one nod. For the first time, they seemed to come to an agreement. Melog sheathed his sword and relaxed his stance. He slid down to the ground and walked his horse over to a nearby tree, where he loosely looped the reins over one of its branches.

Kettle smiled and sighed. "There we are then... all friends, well and good. Now...you know, missy, when we lets you go, you won't be able to hardly see us anymores, and yous certainly won't be able to talks to us. So we'll just wait a bit whilst you get your things together."

"It'll be a long wait," noted Gamliggy.

"For us, not for them," reminded Pitts.

"What? It don't takes us as long to do them things as it does for them?" questioned Gamliggy again.

"No," continued Pitts. "We talked about this. Don't you remember?"

Gamliggy gave this some thought. "Remind me again."

Kettle silently shook his head in frustration.

"Oh, and don't forget the water for that cup of tea, eh?" Gamliggy piped up, apparently forgetting the whole issue about time.

Kettle assumed a serious look. "All right then, mates…are we done? Then let her go!"

"Awww…Kettle," whined Gamliggy, "does we have to?

"Does you want that cup of tea or not? Let her go, Gamliggy," repeated Kettle, looking Cathyn in the eyes. "I thinks we can trust her."

And with that, the grips were loosened, and the three men disappeared, leaving two shimmering blankets of energy hovering in the air on either side of Tempest. Cathyn thought she could still make out their individual faces amidst the wavering blobs.

It took a while for Cathyn or Melog to speak.

Melog walked over to her horse. "You certainly don't aim to honor that agreement, do you?"

Cathyn, dismounting while still eyeing the shimmering figures around them, whispered back, "I do," and walked off to gather some wood for a fire.

CHAPTER 6
A STORY

Within moments the two travelers had a fire going and a pot full of boiling water. Cathyn had scraped out some tea leaves that she had found nearby into the two cups that she had packed and was pouring the water over them. She could sense the now-transparent figures of the three men leaning very closely over her shoulders as she did this.

"Ahem." She cleared her throat. "Do you mind?"

The figures backed away. Cathyn poured the water into the cups and let the tea steep. The steam seemed to be pulled toward the waiting, ghostly men.

"Let's sit," advised Cathyn. "I have a feeling this is going to be a long story."

Captain Melog sighed and remained standing, facing away from them, arms crossed, looking out over the expanse of woods surrounding them.

"Or not," Cathyn sniffed with a glance toward her guide.

"This had better not be a long story," Melog warned over his shoulder, "or I *will* relieve them of their heads."

Cautiously, almost respectfully, the transparent men lined up on two sides of the young warrior—Kettle holding on to Cathyn's upper left arm, with Pitts holding on to Cathyn's right arm, and Gamliggy, just behind Pitts, touching Cathyn's shoulder. With a sharp crackling sound, the ghosts were once again transformed into whole men.

Pitts turned to look up at Captain Melog. "Beggin' your pardon, your lordship, but you don'ts look the type what'd care to be touched in this way."

"Indeed," answered the gray man, and then, mumbling to no one in particular, "I should have cut off their heads when they first appeared."

Ignoring Melog entirely, Gamliggy and Pitts were smiling broadly as they turned to face the fire and caught Cathyn's eye. "Now...hows abouts that tea, mum?" asked Gamliggy.

Cathyn, with the men still attached to various parts of her, picked up the cups off the ground one at a time and handed them to Pitts and Gamliggy. It was a delicate operation; she worked carefully so as to not break contact with any of them.

Pitts and Gamliggy shut their eyes and let the steam roll over their faces. They continued to smile as they breathed in the aroma of the fresh, hot tea. "Nothin' like it," sighed Pitts. "Nothin' in the whole universe like a nice hot cuppa."

"Look at me!" cried Gamliggy. "Know where I am? I'm in heaven, is what." They each took a sip and sighed again.

Gamliggy passed his cup over to Kettle. "Any sugar, mum?" he asked.

"Gamliggy!" Kettle admonished.

"Well, it don't hurt to ask, do it? A bit of sugar makes to sweeten the pot. That's what me grandma used to say."

"Get on with it," hissed Melog.

Kettle turned back to Cathyn. "Nice of you to do this, missy," he whispered. "You have no idea what this means for us." He also took a deep sip and sighed. "It's like bein' reborn all over again, is what it's like." He looked at Gamliggy. "Sugar or no sugar."

"Did you know that cutting off heads is really quite a simple thing to do?" Captain Melog asked aloud as if he were talking to a friend of his who shared his own particular sensibilities.

Kettle's look soured. "You oughta take some time to smell the flowers there, yer lordship. Life is gonna pass you by right quicks-like."

"Not a concern of mine, ghost man," replied the gray rider over his shoulder. Curiously enough, he remained facing away from the prospectors, his back to them.

"What? Life's not a concern of yours?"

"It's what I said."

"Your companion's a cheery one, isn't he?" asked Kettle, giving Cathyn a little wink.

Gamliggy whispered, looking serious, "I don't think he's the flower-smellin' sort, Kettle."

The gray guide sighed and shifted his position.

"We do have to be moving along," reminded Cathyn. "Perhaps you'd best get to your story."

"Mum, you wouldn't happen to have a bite to eat in that pack of yours, would you?" asked Gamliggy. "We gets awful hungry when we're likes this."

"Give you an inch…" began Kettle.

Captain Melog unsheathed his sword.

"It's all right," replied Cathyn. She pulled out some more of the meat and bread and cheese that she had packed, and handed it to Pitts and Gamliggy.

The men both began moaning with each bite that they took. "Every time I do this, it's like it's the first time I've ever eaten in me life!" cried Pitts.

"Well, it is the first time you've eaten in…What do ya think, Pitts? A year?" asked Gamliggy. "Has it been that long, Kettle?"

"Somethin' like that," said Kettle.

"A year!" exclaimed Cathyn. "How can you go without eating for a year? What do you live on?"

"Well, you see, it's like this," Kettle began. "We was prospectin' for lightning gems in these woods here, in the streams."

"Lightning gems?" asked Cathyn.

"Yeah…you never seen 'em, missy? Oh, they're right nice, them lightning gems. They're not like any rock or mineral you've ever seen, more like pure light, they are. Can't even feel 'em in your hands. Just twinklin' little balls of energy, they are, but worth a fortune if'n yous can find 'em. Anyways, we'd heard stories for years about how the rivers and streams here in Abathet Woods was just full of 'em. You could see 'em a-shinin' and a-glintin' in the water, or so they said. We figured if we was to find even a handful of them beauties, why, we could live the good life. Retire. You know, settle down rich and easy-like. Now that I thinks back on it, we must of had the fever awful bad. There's no doubt about it. I know I was half crazy to find them things."

"Me too, Kettle," Gamliggy added. "I was gettin' so's I was dreamin' about lightning gems every night."

Kettle nodded. "Anyways, we hadn't had a stitch of luck, what with all the time we'd spent up here. And so one day, as we was just wakin' up in one of our camps, when what should we see a-comin' through the woods but a line of horses walkin' real slow-like, and there, sittin' on the second horse, a beautiful, big black one, if I recalls correctly, is a lady. She looked to me like a queen of some kind, very regal-like, as they say. Her hair was long and all white, and her skin was all white too, but she weren't old. She were beautiful.

'Ceptin' that her eyes was red. And she wore a thin white cape that hung down almost to her stirrups." Kettle paused to think. "She seemed very surprised to see us."

"Surprised?" piped in Pitts. "She were downright nasty."

"Right, nasty was the look on her face, all right, not happy about us bein' here one bit. I could tell as she looked at us that she was plannin' somethin' already.

"Anyways, I says, 'Good morning, Your Majesty.'

"'And to you,' says she.

"'What brings you to these here parts?' I asks, pretty as you please."

"You always did have good manners, Kettle," added Gamliggy.

"Thank you. I've always thought so."

"Does you remember that time last year when that trader was passin' through?" Gamliggy began.

"Cutting off heads!" the guide roared.

Kettle looked at Captain Melog's back, then over to Gamliggy. "Where was I?"

"You was as pretty as you please," replied Gamliggy. "I loves this story," he added, giving Cathyn a knowing wink.

"Right. As pretty as you please. So she says, 'I might ask the same of you.'

"'Oh,' says I, 'we're just lowly prospectors, Your Majesty. It's lightning gems what we're after. Do you happen to know where there might be a run of 'em around here?'

"'Lightning gems?' says she, smiling a little. I remember her smiling a little at that. It was a strange kind of smile."

"Right nasty smile, if you asks me," added Gamliggy.

"So she smiles, see. And then she says, 'I believe you've been duped by rumor. There are no lightning gems in these parts.'

"'So we're findin' out,' says I.

"'And what will you do now, prospector?' she asks.

"'Well,' says I, 'I believe we be throwin' in the pick and shovel, as they say, Your Majesty.' 'Cause it's here, you see, that I'm beginnin' to get a bad feelin' about Her Majesty, what with that nasty smile and all. So… this is where I starts my bowin' and smilin' pretty as a picture and backin' away slow-like, and I says, 'It's high time we went home, Your Majesty. No gems for these prospectors.'

"And now here's where it starts to go bad, you see, because this whole time she hasn't stopped smiling, not a smidge."

"And them dark red eyes," added Gamliggy. "Like rat's eyes."

"And Her Majesty, she just keeps a-lookin' at me, and she says, 'I don't think so, prospector.'

"'Your Majesty?' says I, pretending not to know what she's talkin' about.

"'I say I cannot let you leave,' says she.

"'And...why would that be, Your Majesty?' I asks.

"'Well,' says she, 'for one thing, you've displeased me. You are stealing from my lands.'

"'Your lands?' I asks. 'These woods belongs to you?'

"'These are Abathet Woods, are they not?' she asks.

"'They are, Your Majesty.'

"'And I am Lady Abathet, am I not?' says she.

"Now, I can feels me heart poundin' in me chest and the hairs on the backs of me neck risin' up—"

"And you gots a lot of those," interrupted Gamliggy.

Kettle gave Gamliggy a serious look.

"You know, hairs," continued Gamliggy, figuring that his friend did not understand the statement.

"Heads!"

Kettle looked back at Cathyn and continued. "So I'm gettin' nervous-like 'cause we've heard of Lady Abathet, see—one of the dark warrior sorceresses that are supposed to have walked the world for over a hundred lifetimes. She's infamous where we come from, and most feared."

"And we thought she was dead," continued Pitts. "That's why we figured it was safe to enter the woods in the first place."

"'And for another thing,' she goes on, 'you've seen me alive.'

"So I drops down to one knee, like, in a sign of respect, and bows me head low, and I says, 'It's all our fault, Your Majesty. We shouldna oughta been up in these here woods. I'm sure if you'll just… let us go home, you won't have a thing to worry about.'

"I tilts me head a wee bit and opens one eye to see if me message is gettin' across-like. She's still smiling that sick smile of hers and lookin' at us.

"'No, prospector,' says she, 'this will be your home from now on. Your tactfulness and deference have saved your lives, but I cannot let you tell others that you've seen me alive and afoot. Perhaps the best thing for you three is…to get a little closer to the lightning gems that you seek.'

"And with that she lifts her arms up in the air and says somethin' in a language none of us has ever heard before, and we hears a loud bang and a cracklin' sound and then—"

"Everythin' looks…different," finished Gamliggy, moving his open hand in the air around him.

Kettle looked at his one hand that was holding the metal cup. He passed the cup back to Gamliggy. "All of a sudden, the sky and the trees and everythin' around us goes all dark, and we notice that the horses and the people on 'em are moving real slow, like they was in water, trying to dash their ways out. And we can hear 'em talkin', but it's real slow, too—just moanin' and groanin' is all it sounds like to us."

"What did she do to you?" asked Cathyn.

"Near as we can figure it," piped in Pitts, eyeing Melog and his sword hand, "she kind of turned us into lightning gem people...sped up our bodies so that we're goin' fast-like while everythin' else around us is movin' real slow. That's why we can't touch anythin'. We're vibratin' too fast. Things around us just passin' right through us as if we was ghosts. We can even walk through the trees here as if they was nothin', if'n we thinks hard about it."

"But we did discover that if'n we touched a livin' thing, we'd slow down long enough to appreciate our old slow bodies," added Gamliggy.

"That's why you don't have to eat anything," whispered Cathyn.

"Right," continued Kettle. "We're never hungry until we're slowed down. And it's right rare that anyone comes through these woods for us to touch 'em and slow us down."

"I tried grabbin' a bunny once," sniffed Pitts. "Slowed me down a little, but I scared the poor thing so. Haven't done that since."

"That's also why we didn't grab the horses, mum," continued Kettle. "It scares animals somethin' fierce."

"What about touching the trees?" suggested Cathyn. "They're alive."

"We tried that," answered Pitts. "It don't seem to work with them. Not the right kind of aliveness."

Gamliggy got a faraway look in his eyes. "I thinks it has somethin' to do with relativity."

"What does?" asked Pitts.

"How we moves at different speeds and all."

The others looked at Gamliggy in an odd way.

"Relativywhat?" asked Kettle.

Captain Melog stabbed his long sword into the ground.

"It's just somethin' I gots a feeling about," Gamliggy continued. "It come to me one day in a daydream. It's like energy things like us and light and then the real, solid world—we all works together, but different. You see, it all depends on which side you're on for it to make a difference. And it's all different depending on which side you're lookin' out from. But it all works together, too, you see. It's like energy and solid things is the same thing, in a way...but different." Gamliggy's voice trailed off.

The quizzical looks on everyone's faces did not change.

"Look, it's like this...Supposin' you're an energy thing like us, and you're runnin' along on a horse that's made up of energy just like you."

"A lightning horse!" piped up Pitts.

"I know. Wouldn't you just love to have one of those?" Gamliggy smiled.

A low growl could be heard coming from Captain Melog.

There was a slight pause, and Gamliggy continued with his thought. "So, you're ridin' this lightnin' horse, see, but then there's one of you solid blokes standin' nearby watchin' us run by and timin' us, like."

The gray rider looked up into the sky beseechingly. "For the love of horses!"

Cathyn brought them back to the story. "But why can't you leave these woods?"

"Well, just as Lady Abathet and her party is a-startin' to go, she leans down from her horse, real close-like to us, and she says, clear as a bell, 'This is your home now, lightning men. The center of your energy is here. Try to leave, and you will dissipate into the air like seeds from a dandylion.' And then they was gone."

"So you're prisoners," whispered Cathyn.

"Right you are, missy," said Pitts. "Prisoners it is. And cursed prisoners at that!"

Cathyn was quiet. She looked at the men as they finished the teacups and passed them back. "I've got...a place that I've got to go to. After I've done what I've come to do, I'll return here and help you three break the curse that Lady Abathet has put on you."

"Fine thoughts, missy," whispered Kettle. "We thank you for them fine thoughts, but no one's ever come back for us."

"We've told our story before, mum," added Pitts, "but no one's ever come back."

"Probably because you bored them to death," mumbled Captain Melog between clenched teeth.

"Well…" She paused. "I'll come back. If I can. If I'm still alive. I'll come back."

The three prospectors took this in silently.

"Right!" interjected Cathyn's guide suddenly without turning around. "We've heard the story, and now it's time to go. Don't try to touch her again while we're crossing through the forest, or I will touch you, and then you will lose your heads." He resheathed his sword and began walking toward where the horses were tethered.

Kettle looked hard at Cathyn. "I have half a mind to believe you, missy. There's somethin' special in your eyes, if'n yous don't mind me sayin'."

"I don't mind. Thank you for that. I was beginning to have some doubts myself. Well…" She paused. "Good-bye." She waited for them to break contact. For some reason, it seemed rude to break the contact herself.

Kettle gave Gamliggy and Pitts a serious look, and the three of them let go, crackled, and buzzed into the open air.

"Thanks for the tea, mum," she heard as the lightning men dissolved before her.

Cathyn cleared the camp and caught up with Captain Melog, who was now on his white stallion and sauntering farther along into the forest. She repacked her saddlebag and mounted Tempest, following closely behind him.

The riders appeared to be alone. They weren't. Three transparent figures were constantly standing nearby talking to one another. They were able to catch up to the two travelers and stand well ahead of them at many different points in their passage.

"Did you see what I seen?" asked Kettle.

"I did at that, Kettle," whispered Gamliggy. And then, "What did you see?"

"That bloke in black and gray with the sword," answered Kettle.

"His lordship? What about him?" asked Pitts. "Seemed to me he needed a good lesson in manners. Had some issues about cutting things, if'n you knows what I mean." He touched his neck.

"No, didn't you recognize him?" asked Kettle.

"No. We seen him before?" asked Pitts.

"We seen him before," answered Kettle. "He was the first one on horseback when Lady Abathet came through here with that ridin' party of hers. Looked to me like he was her second-in-command."

CHAPTER 7

THE MURDERED MAN

They were almost outside of Abathet Woods. The full cover of trees was thinning out, revealing an open but clouded sky. It was beginning to grow dark. Already constellations were swinging into position overhead. Cathyn talked as they rode.

"I can't find any stars that I know," Cathyn whispered to no one in particular.

"You're not likely to, dear heart," replied Captain Melog. "These are stars of another time, another place."

He continued looking out ahead of them, pivoting his head and body slowly so that he could get a full view around them. Listening hard.

"I read somewhere that stars sometimes turn into other kinds of celestial bodies," whispered Cathyn, "that things happen to them."

Melog still did not look at her. "Yes, things happen to them," he said. "Some stars are known to turn."

He held his head up high as if smelling the air around them. He did not look comfortable. The horses were starting to jostle as they stepped.

"What's wrong?" Cathyn whispered.

"I...don't know. The horses can smell something." He was quiet, listening. "Stay mounted, but arm yourself. We'll at least have higher ground. It might be grasshounds."

Cathyn slowly unsheathed her longsword from its scabbard. The blade caught parts of the newly forming stars in the sky and glistened when she turned it. A beautiful sword, really. She hardened her fingers around the grip and focused all of her attention to her hearing. Tempest had stopped, but now moved slightly backward and to the side. He was obviously worried.

A rustling in the bushes and the trees to their left.

The thing leaped at Cathyn, knocking her from her horse. It was all dark and fur-covered and snarling. Before she had a chance to skewer it with her sword, she felt it hovering above her. When she looked, Captain Melog, still on his stallion, had his sword in the nape of its neck and was flinging it to one side. Three other creatures appeared to their right now. Cathyn wasted no time in arming herself with her bow. Getting herself into a kneeling position, she fired off two quick shots, taking out two of the monsters. Melog was riding over to the third. A deft swing of his sword took the head off of it. He hacked at two more that showed up to reinforce the attack. Cathyn could see that they were like the wild hounds that she knew back home, but heavier, covered more completely in a dark, almost black, fur. Their ears were more pointed, tall, and sharp-edged. They obviously hunted in packs. They seemed both intelligent and malicious. Cathyn got off one more arrow. Another creature had suddenly appeared. She hit it in the neck. It howled and ran back into the undergrowth. It would be dead within moments.

And just as suddenly as it had begun, it ended. No more creatures emerged from the trees. The two travelers remained silent, listening.

After twenty or so heartbeats, Melog said, "They're gone. We were obviously too much for them. Not what they expected."

He looked at Cathyn, who had stood up by now. Her face beggged a question. "Grasshounds," he answered her. "They're particularly vicious in this part of our world."

Cathyn breathed a deep sigh and sheathed her longsword. She dusted herself off, walked over to the two creatures that she had taken down, and pulled her mother's arrows from their bodies. She wiped them off on her pants and then put them back in the quill on her back. She then walked over to Tempest, who had shied away from the danger. It was a miracle that none of the creatures had attacked him. Cathyn reassured her horse and mounted again.

Captain Melog trotted over to where they were regaining their land legs. "Are you hurt?"

"No," Cathyn reassured him. "Just shaken."

They were silent. They had both defended themselves and each other. An interesting dynamic considering the previously untrusting bond between them.

Melog took the moment to turn his horse and move on. He was not going to permit them to be sitting targets again to whatever was out there. He took the reins in his left hand. His sword was in his right, facing straight up into the sky. Cathyn followed behind.

Full nighttime had finally come upon them when they looked around and realized that they had reached the true end of the woods. The moon was now bright and full just behind some fast-moving dark clouds directly above them. The brightness of the moon turned the cloud cover into a beautiful light blue blanket.

The riders emerged from a last copse of trees, into a clearing of mostly rocks and grasses. The clearing was bordered by thick trees and bushes on either side, but there was a stream nearby. They were definitely on a plateau of some kind; the ground hinted of a downward slope just on the other side of the stream. It had been a little while since they had heard any more rustling in the woods. The grasshounds that had been tracking them earlier had, obviously, moved on to other prey.

"We'll stop here," Melog stated and dismounted. He led his own horse over to the running water to drink.

Cathyn did the same. They had been traveling for an entire day now, a day filled with wondrous and terrible things, and it was late. She realized that she was truly tired.

She pulled her pack from the back of the saddle, unrolled two blankets onto a spot near the stream, and sat down cross-legged on them. She rummaged around for something to eat. She found some fruit and cheese and a flat piece of bread, and she began eating that.

"I'm too tired to fix a fire, Melog," she sighed.

"A fire may keep away any more grasshounds," he whispered. His voice echoed into the night. They could both hear the sound of their horses thirstily lapping up the cold water.

"I think we're safe here," Cathyn replied. "The horses don't seem worried anymore." She paused and sighed resignedly. "But perhaps you're right."

She started a small fire using the flint stones that she had brought along, bordering it with three large rocks that she had found nearby. Starting a fire was always like trying to bring someone back to life. A very delicate process. A cautious affair. You could lose the patient at any time. She placed her one pot on top of the rocks and the now-roaring fire and began putting in the remainder of her meats. She added some roots that she had dug up nearby, some edible leaves and flower parts, and some water from the stream. Throwing in a dash of spices, she soon had a reasonable stew brewing. She scooped out a spoonful, blew on it, and tasted. Delicious. So good out in the open, under the stars. She was going to offer a spoonful to her guide and then stopped herself.

When Cathyn finished her meal, she went over to the stream to wash out the pot. Lifting the water in and out of the pot, she noticed something white lying at the bottom of the streambed. Picking it up out of the water, she saw that it was a bone. It looked human. Perhaps a finger bone. It made her shiver. She slipped it back into the water and looked cautiously around her. This was not a good place.

Cathyn put a large assortment of oats and grasses in the pot and offered it to Tempest, who started to eat gratefully. She petted the horse on the neck, gave him an apple that she had found on the ground nearby, whispered something endearing to him, and tethered him to a tree. She noticed that Captain Melog never talked to his horse, never even acknowledged it. Perhaps that was part of the way they treated horses in this world. She removed Tempest's saddle and saddle blankets and wiped him down so that he was dry for the night.

Presently, Cathyn stretched out on her own blankets. She began to meditate as her mother had taught her to do, a practice that all warriors engaged in before sleep.

She let all of the muscles in her body roll away from her. She aimed her inner focus at the sound of her own breathing. Gradually, she could detect her heartbeat slowing down. She began to focus on the circle rhyme that each warrior must come up with. It was a unique device for each person. It helped the body relax and prepare the warrior for the following day, especially if the following day was a day scheduled for battle. The effect was to lose herself out of herself. She became completely connected to her body, and then a separate entity from her body. It was almost a floating or a flying experience. The body was left behind and the mind or the soul (or whatever it was that was inside of her) traveled.

My flesh is the crust of the mountain.

My blood is the river that flows.

My breath is the wind of the heavens.

My thoughts are the words of the old.

She saw in her mind's eye a bright field. She was riding Tempest through this field, tall, golden grain, ready to be harvested all about them. This was one of her favorite meditation visions. She could hear Tempest's hard breathing competing with her own as they galloped fast through the golden landscape. She clutched his mane and held on. They were both confident and happy. They caressed each other's thoughts.

Then her mind suddenly turned black. It made her body, still prone on the blankets, shudder, though she did not know it. She was now walking in the clearing in which they were camped. She was looking around her on all sides; obviously something was amiss. An anxious feeling of dread and foreboding welled up deep inside of her. She did not like this new meditation. She would try hard to change it around, force it to a lighter, happier scene.

Cathyn turned suddenly, sure that there was something behind her. A man was standing, half in shadow, ten meters away from her, just standing and looking at her in the dark of the forest. It made her shudder. She would have drawn her sword if it weren't just a meditative vision. Best to just see this out and figure out what it meant. Perhaps it was here to tell her something, give her a warning of some kind. She blinked, and he was one meter closer. She blinked again, and he was closer still. By the third blink, he was face-to-face with her.

A brown hood was pulled up over the back of his head, but Cathyn could see that his face was a ghostly white, and there were long, fat veins running down his cheeks and along his neck. He looked like he had been ill for a very long time and, somewhere along the line, he had become totally insane. He was clean-shaven, but his hair was very long; it cascaded out of his hood and down his shoulders. His face was expressionless. He seemed to look at her closely more out of curiosity than anything else. He was dressed in the same kind of hunting or trading clothes as she was, but they were old and tattered, full of holes. She could make out a large splotch of blood on his chest. A foul-smelling drool dripped off of the man's lips and onto the ground.

The hooded man almost seemed to smile. It revealed yellowed and cracked teeth. "This is not a dream," he whispered. He seemed surprised and tilted his head. He was studying her.

Cathyn did not like this dark vision, but she accepted visions like this one when they came along; they were a part of the warrior lessons that she had studied at the Academy. The trick was to face whatever fears presented themselves, deal with them, and then learn something from them.

"What do you want?" she asked cautiously. She hoped she was putting on a good show.

The hooded man stopped smiling. "Your soul," he answered.

Cathyn backed away, and the man disappeared. She felt a cold breath on her shoulder. Now he was behind her. She turned around. He had his hands on her shoulders. Cathyn was shocked. Nothing in her meditations had ever touched her before. She moved her arms in a hard windmill motion, breaking off his hold. He disappeared again. This time she saw him over by the tree where the horses had been tethered. The horses were gone, as was Captain Melog. This was her fight and hers alone.

She looked around her and noticed that she was back near her blankets. She reached for her bow, nocked an arrow, and let it fly. It hit the ghostly figure in the right arm, pinning him to the tree.

He didn't scream, just moved his arm forward along the shaft of the arrow until it exited out where the fletchings were. There was no sign of blood or injury. He ran toward her, arms out wide, growling.

Cathyn dropped her bow, picked up her longsword, and swung it at the ragged figure. He smiled and ducked. She swung again. He stepped out of the way. She plunged the sword into the center of his chest and pulled it away. He showed no reaction. There was no sign of blood on the blade. He was not alive, but it was clear that he could hurt her if given the opportunity.

He had Cathyn on the defensive. She continued backing away, still swinging her sword. She would slice at his hand, and it would fly into the air, only to be still attached when next Cathyn looked. She would slice off his head, and then blink once, and it was back. He seemed to be impervious to her weapons. She kept slicing off parts of him as he rushed toward her. She would blink, and he would be whole again. She was almost running backward at this point.

Then she remembered the bone she had picked out of the water in the stream.

The rabid man was still coming at her at full speed. "Kiss me, and it will all be over," he hissed. His eyes still looked insane.

"That's not going to happen!" she yelled back.

Cathyn suddenly changed course and charged straight ahead at the lunatic. Knocking him to the ground, she continued on until she came to the stream. She stopped at the place where she had found the finger bone before and looked. There, just a man's height from the first sighting, was a small pile of bones, some scattered throughout the bottom of the streambed by animals and currents, but all white and washed clean by the running water. They were much more present here in this meditation than in the real world. It was as if they had been newly gathered and placed there. She took her longsword and rammed it right into the center of the bone pile.

"No!" he screamed, and froze where he stood, arms stretched straight out from his body.

She said nothing, just stood next to her sword that rose from the water now like a planted flag of conquest. For some reason, Cathyn knew that, as long as her sword stayed pierced in the bone pile, he was powerless.

"Who are you?" she whispered, calm now.

"I...I...am the Murdered Man," he said quietly. He tried to move, but he could not. There was a look of shock and disbelief on his face. "How can this be?"

"What's your name?"

The man looked wide-eyed and worried now. "I… don't remember," he sighed. He looked at the sword in surrender.

"Is all of this real?" she asked.

He looked back at Cathyn. "It is in your mind. I entered it when you were sleeping."

"Why did you do that?"

"I hunt for souls now," he whispered. "I enter travelers' minds at night, and I take their souls when they're sleeping."

"Why?"

"Because…" He seemed to not know the answer. "I was murdered here."

Cathyn looked again at the blood on the man's chest. "How long ago?" she asked.

The ghoul shook his head back and forth, looked down at the ground. "So long ago. So long ago. I hunt at night now, when the sun disappears and the moon becomes full."

"Who killed you?"

The ghost looked up at her again. "Another trader. My partner." The fury returned to his once-wild eyes. "We had stones of silver. So many. We were on our way to be rich. He stabbed me"—he looked down at his chest—"and left my body in this stream. I walk the earth here now."

Cathyn mulled this over. "I wasn't sleeping," she explained. "I was meditating. That is why I can fight back."

The ghost considered this.

"I will wake myself up from my meditation," she said. "I will bury your bones over by that tree." She nodded her head in the direction of a large acorn tree on the other side of the stream. "You will need to find your way home after that."

"Home?" the ghoul repeated.

"Yes. Home. You can do that now. Your bones will be buried. I will say some words."

"What words could help me?" the ghost whimpered.

"These words will...remember you. They will help guide you," she whispered.

Still standing by the sword, she closed her eyes and willed herself to wake up. It was safe now. The Murdered Man could not move. She took the transition slowly, working her way back into her body from her feet and her legs and then moving up to her torso and arms and head. It was like resurfacing from a deep depth of water.

She was back on her blankets, lying flat on her back. She sat up. The sounds of the forest and the wind and the stream brought her back to reality. This was the real world, at least one real world out of, apparently, many. Captain Melog was still tending to his horse. Tempest was still sleeping by the stream. Nothing had been touched here. All was calm. She stood up and walked over to the water. She opened up her now-empty cloth food bag and began scooping in all of the bones that she could find in the streambed. She found a swollen spot in the bottom mud and dug at that. A skull appeared. When it looked like she had gotten most of the bones, she hopped over the stream, took out her knife, and began stabbing at the ground near the foot of the tree.

"What are you doing?" Melog questioned her.

"Taking care of some forgotten business," she replied. No need to tell him of this.

Melog went back to caring for his horse.

When she was finished with the hole, she carefully placed the bones inside, covered them up, then said something quietly over the "grave."

"You are no longer the Murdered Man," she whispered to the bones. "You are who you once were. You are free to go home. Look for the ones who love you. They'll help you to go home." She didn't know what else to say. Perhaps that was all that was necessary. She sighed and stood up.

Cathyn walked back over to her fire, stretched her arms into the air, and repositioned herself on the blankets. She listened lazily to the sounds of the wind far away and all around them. The gurgling of the water in the stream nearby was comforting. It seemed to be hovering over her, waiting to drop on her like a spiderweb across her face. And then, at long last, she was truly asleep.

CHAPTER 8

IN SYMPATHY

She awoke to a noise that did not sound right. A humming sound…behind her.

"Hmmmmmmmmmmmm…"

She turned around. "Melog, what is that?"

Looking up, she noticed that Captain Melog was gone. There was no trace of her guide. Had he gone out walking and guarding, or had he just left her? It was nearly morning, parts of the sky almost a dark green as it slid from the blue black of night. She had slept the remainder of the night away.

"Hmmmmmmmmmmm…" Again, this time to her left.

She turned.

"Hmmmmmmmmmwhoareyou?" a humming voice asked in the dark to her right. It was all said in a steady, low monotone. And then the sound of a thud.

"What?" cried Cathyn. She felt for her shin sheath, pulled out her knife. "If it's not one thing, it's another."

Again, behind her, in the dark. "Hmmmmmmmmmwhoareyou?"Thud.

Cathyn was up on her knees, knife in hand. She dared not speak again. She listened for a place to strike.

"Hmmmmmmmmwhoareyou?"Thud.

"Cathyn," she answered finally, barely a whisper.

Another humming voice came from another direction, followed by another thud.

"HmmmmmCathynisthenameyouuseattheend?" Thud.

"What?"

"HmmmmmmmmmCathynisthenameyouuse attheend?" the other voice repeated. Thud.

Judging by the voices that came at her from all directions, she was surrounded. And those thudding noises.

Were they hitting the ground with sticks, weapons? She could not make out solid bodies in the changing light. More lightning men? Whatever they were, they seemed invisible. Even with her waking eyesight coming into focus, she couldn't see them. What did they mean by the name she used at the end? Of course.

"No, Cathyn is my first name."

"HmmmmmmmmmmCathynisthenameyouuseatthe start?" Thud.

"Yes…Cathyn. The name I use at the end is Bood." She put down her knife and slowly reached over to where her sword lay flat on the ground. She'd need something to use at close quarters, something deadlier than her knife. She rested her hand on the grip of her sword. She could hear no reaction from the voices around her. She slowly brought the sword up into her lap.

Now Cathyn was aware of an intense spinning going on all around her. There seemed to be small objects twirling in the air. She could see that now. She got on her knees and lifted her sword up into a striking pose. A target could be hit with just a sound. And the spinning sounds were certainly loud enough. Where was Melog?

"Hmmmmmmmmwhatisthenameitusesatthestart—"

"Cathyn...I told you."

"Hmmmmmmmmmletmefinish...Hmmmmmmm thenameitusesatthestartofitsmother?"Thud.

Cathyn thought about this. It was like a riddle. "The name at the start of my mother?"

"HmmmmmmmmmthatiswhatIsaid."Thud.

"My mother's name is Kaal Bood."

Suddenly, all around her on all sides, Cathyn could hear the sound of furious spinning and voices. The voices became a chant.

"Hmmmmm Kaal Bood... Hmmmmmmm Kaal Bood... Hmmmmmmm Kaal Bood... HmmmmmmmKaalBood..."Thud.

By now the light had changed. The night was gone. What could she see?

Small, flat objects in the air all around her, flying, jumping. No, not just jumping. They were spinning… or a combination of both. There seemed to be twenty or thirty of them. They were like little rocks, smooth, flat gray stones that, when they spun, hung in the air and then dropped to the ground with a slight thud when the spin wore out. Is that how they talked, when the air around them was disturbed by the spinning? Did they do this when the sun came up? They looked like toads jumping all around her in an effort to catch insects.

The chanting stopped, and the spinning rocks came to rest. A moment of silence followed. Cathyn held her breath.

Suddenly, one lone stone shot up in front of her and dangled in the air, spinning furiously. As it talked, Cathyn could just make out a kind of squashed face within the blurring motion—two open eyes, a wide, pressed mouth, one small hole for a nose.

"Hmmmmmmyouareinsympathy." Thud.

"Sympathy?"

"Hmmmmmmharmony." Thud.

"What do you mean?" She relaxed her grip on the sword.

"Hmmmmmmmitspresencedoesushonor." Thud.

"My presence? Why?"

"HmmmmmmmKaalBood." Thud.

"My mother."

"HmmmmmmmmKaalBood." And, once more, all the other stone singers joined in on that same humming chorus.

"HmmmmmmmmKaalBood…Hmmmmmmmm KaalBood…HmmmmmmmmKaalBood…" Then the sound of many thuds hitting the ground.

After a slight pause, it started again.

"Hmmmmmmmmtherearemanyofuswhoarein rebellion."Thud.

"Rebellion? Rebellion against whom?"

And then, one lone spinning voice. "Hmmmmmmmm danger."

A series of thuds cut off the talking. Cathyn was now aware of the horses moving about where they were tethered.

"What kind of danger?" Cathyn whispered at last.

Again, silence. And then, "Hmmmmmmmm dangerisnear."Thud.

Another one. "Hmmmmmmmmsheisnear." Thud.

Cathyn thought about this. "'She' as in me? Or 'she' as in my mother?" And then one last thought came to her. "Or 'she' as in someone else is near to me? Someone…another 'she'…is dangerous?"

"Hmmmmmmmmanothershe."Thud.

"Hmmmmmmmmanothersheisdanger."Thud.

Quiet again. And then, "Hmmmmmmmmanother shehaswhatyouneed."Thud.

"Hmmmmmmmmanothersheneedswhatyouhave."
Thud.

Another riddle. "She has what I need, and she needs
what I have," Cathyn interpreted.

"HmmmmmmmmmthatiswhatIsaid."Thud.

"Hmmmmmmmmsheisnear...Hmmmmmmmm
sheisnear...Hmmmmmmmmsheisnear...
Hmmmmmmmmsheisnear."

And just as suddenly, the singing voices stopped
spinning and all the stones dropped in unison to the
ground with loud, intermittent thuds, like a hard rain,
or a volley of arrows piercing the earth. All was silence
around her.

Cathyn reached down and picked up one of the
stones. It was cold and smooth. There was no vibration
or movement of any kind, nor was there now a face.
She turned the stone over and over in her hand as if it
would help unlock the now-missing face.

"I heard something," Captain Melog's voice cut
through the quiet.

Cathyn turned to see the guide standing just
behind her, looking curiously into the air in front of
her. "Melog! Where did you go?"

"I was scouting. On guard. Grasshounds are known
to attack in the early hours of the day. I thought I heard
voices." He was looking now at the fallen stones.

"You keep doing this to me," Cathyn whispered
between clenched teeth. "I can't tell if you're setting

me up for a trap or if you want me to find out something. I know you don't want me killed."

Captain Melog raised his eyebrows. "I've told you what my job is, dear heart. It would not be in my best interest to lose you to a grasshound or a—"

His voice was cut off by the sound of Cathyn rising up and swinging her longsword toward Melog. In just as fast a movement, he had drawn his own sword and was countering her thrusts. Seven times she hacked at him, from the left, the right, above, the right again, an uppercut swing. Each swing as fast as half a heartbeat. He slowly and meticulously took a step back, defending himself against the blows, sword to sword, like he was taking practice. He did not seem excited or worried about the attack. Just caught in the process of defending himself. He would have liked to take it to the next level as soon as she tired, but he knew he could not. Above all else, he must return with her alive.

Cathyn's swordplay was no match for the experienced and disciplined Melog, but her fury and sudden attack were on her side. Eventually the dark guide stopped stepping backward and allowed her to end the volley with her sword blade angled against his neck, his own sword between them both. She could smell his skin. It was not anything that Cathyn had ever smelled before.

"Don't think about crossing me, Melog," she growled low between her teeth. "If this is a trap, and I make it out alive, I promise you, I'll find you wherever you are, and my arrows will hit you on two marks: one in the center of your head, and the other in your heart."

Captain Melog smiled. He swung his sword in a downward and lightning-fast arc. It took Cathyn's sword with it as well, embedding it, point first, into the ground, her hand still on the hilt. The movement was so fast, Cathyn almost stumbled in her effort to hold on to it. She dared not look away from his face.

"I wish you well then," he whispered. "If, by the end of this little escapade, you are in a position to realize both of those targets, then, by all means…you'll have earned them. Dear heart."

Five or six heartbeats passed between the two of them.

"Regardless," Melog spoke as he turned and walked back to the stream, "we need to go."

He began saddling his horse for the trip down the mountain. It was as if nothing had happened.

CHAPTER 9

DOWN

It was now daytime, but the sky was still very dark with threatening thunderclouds moving swiftly across it.

Cathyn folded her blankets and repacked her satchel. She went to check on Tempest and saddle him up.

When she mounted her horse, she saw Melog on his own stallion, staring now at a line of trees and rocks that looked like the starting point of their descent down the mountain. Cathyn could see, straight ahead of her, tiny patches of dark blue sky poking out in between the lush branches of the trees. Captain Melog had said the journey would take one day, one night, and part of another day. And now here it was, the morning of the next day. Would she see her mother soon? She could feel her heart in her chest. She took a deep breath and urged Tempest on, behind Captain Melog, and down the slope.

The path was very steep at points. Melog led the way, his stallion placing its hooves in a slow dance that safely moved them from one natural landing to another. They continued this single-file routine in silence until they reached a fifth landing. The angle of descent was straightening out. There was one more face to climb down to get to solid ground, but now Cathyn could see for miles ahead of her.

They had left the closeness of the forest behind and above them. They were now on an overlook staring out at a wide gray sky and, more impressively, an enormous ocean. A strong sea wind blew Cathyn's long black hair out away from her face. She had known before that she was not in her own world. Now she was sure of it. There was not supposed to be an ocean here, or anywhere nearby where she lived, for that matter, certainly not within a day's ride. She had, of course, heard of oceans before. Indeed, her mother had once told her about a famous one called Havagus Ocean.

It was located along the western coast of the country. Merchants from other lands would dock at some of the bigger ports there, Nothsham, Crescent, Foressdurn. Those cities seemed to Cathyn to be the centers of the world—so exciting, so diverse, with mystery and adventure possible with every new enterprise.

According to one of the ocean stories, a pirate ship had pulled up into Crescent one day with a load of spices and teas. No one ever knew where the pirates had come from, just that they were there from out of nowhere one day.

Their ship was very foreign-looking, a three-masted schooner, one tall mast in the aft and two smaller ones in the center and front. The masts were rigged with black and red sails, secured tightly once it was pulling into port.

The ship itself was made of a darkly stained and laminated wood that none of the merchants and seamen could identify. They flew no flag. They seemed an uncivilized lot, dirty and rough and dressed in dark and ragged clothing. But they followed the rules and regulations of the city and the Order of Merchant Ships, and they gave no one any trouble. At least in the beginning. Besides, the spices and teas were new to the people of Crescent; they could be known to turn a blind eye, if necessary, in order to experience something original and different, something that could change their lives for the better, especially where new food was concerned.

One of the pirates in particular stuck out in the merchants' eyes. He was a small, mysterious-looking man dressed in long black robes. He appeared out of the quarterdeck and walked along the centerboard to the stern, watching the rest of the crew trade and sell their goods that they had brought along. Many of the merchants remember seeing the other crew members, now on the dock, looking astonished and scared that the man had emerged from the captain's quarters, like he shouldn't have gotten out. They stopped what they were doing and looked up at the bow of the ship with grave worry and concern.

The little man had a wild look in his eyes. Many said he looked to be insane. He smiled and turned his gaze on as much of the city of Crescent that he could see from the dark ship. Many of the other pirates started calling up after him and yelling. They left their wares on the dock and began frantically running up the walkway to the main deck. The small man seemed to pay them little mind, just continued smiling in a satisfied manner and looking at the city around him, his eyes wild and bright.

He then pulled out a red cloth from within his cloak. Some people thought that it was stained with blood. He placed it on the piping along the front of the ship. He closed his eyes and looked to be making a prayer or an incantation of some sort over the cloth. Then he took the red cloth in his hands and gave it one great shake as though he were dusting it out. It made a snapping sound. A long red mist began issuing from the cloth. It poured over the bow and down onto the dock and the lapping seawater like steam from a teapot. It surrounded the men and women who had come to look and sell and buy. Through the red mist, the onlookers could see the small man being grabbed and forced down onto the deck by the other pirates. After a while, the mist began to take shape. When it had dissipated, there stood on the dock a dragon almost the size of the ship that had brought it to Crescent. The dragon went mad and killed all those who stood in its path as it made its way up to where the rest of the people lived, and eventually into the mountains, where they say it still lives to this day. The Crescent Dragon. Those who were left alive remember seeing the ship unfurl its sails and silently move back out to the ocean, leaving the dragon behind to destroy the city.

Cathyn squinted as she looked out at this new ocean. She could almost imagine a black schooner far out on the horizon line.

A red-tailed hawk suddenly appeared, floating on the wind at face-level with the young warrior. It was hovering so close, Cathyn thought that she could reach out and touch the bird. It made eye contact with her and screeched as it tried to maintain its balance on the unstable ocean breeze. It banked its wings and headed inland toward the trees and the mountain.

It had started to rain—light, airy drops that were more like spray. Cathyn got her cloak out of her bag and put it on. She pulled up her hood. She could taste the salt in the air. Melog touched her shoulder and pointed down. They continued on.

They couldn't see the sun, but they figured that, by the way the light was reflecting off of the ocean, it was before noon. They reached the foot of the mountain and hit sandy beach.

The horses loved the wide openness of the beach. They staggered in the soft sand that was near the foot of the mountain until they came to the more densely packed sand near the water. It was raining harder now. Cathyn clutched at the cloak around her neck. Captain Melog rode just ahead of her. They were moving along a slight curve, following the natural formation of the mountain as it wound in an arc next to the ocean.

Suddenly, Captain Melog kicked his horse into a hard gallop. Of course. Neither of the horses had had a chance to really run themselves out. It had been a walking and trotting journey the whole way up until now. Cathyn did the same.

Tempest relished the power that the run gave him. Cathyn could almost feel the horse laughing under her body. She knew he was happy. He was in paradise running full-out and feeling the rain on his face. Riders oftentimes speak of being able to feel joy when it is present in the horse that they are riding. That was the case here. They kept up this gallop for a few kilometers, both riders passing one another as each horse surged forward. Melog's stallion was a powerful runner. To someone watching from afar, it would have looked as though a race were on.

Tempest finally tired out and slowed to a trot. Cathyn was nearly out of breath. She often shared in the work that Tempest put forth. She could see Captain Melog up ahead also slowing to a steady trot.

The woman warrior pulled her salt-and-pepper up to a halt and slid down into the sand. She walked over toward the ocean. Tempest walked loyally alongside of her. She had never felt the ocean on her feet. She took off her boots and let the cold water glide on and off her legs as the tide wound its way up along the shore.

There was a small island just about three kilometers out in the water, to their left. A wild foam had been worked up in the ocean between the island and the riders. When Cathyn looked closer, she saw that the foam was full of horses, wild horses of different colors that were now swimming toward the beach. It took Cathyn's breath away. The power that the horses demonstrated in their wild swimming was palpable. Tempest saw it as well. They both stopped to watch.

Eventually, the first wave of horses rose up onto the sand and shook themselves dry, prancing back and forth, obviously exhilarated by the swim. Their coats were long and matted, but still beautiful. Cathyn had always appreciated the beauty of horses, but these were stunning. And then she knew; this was where Captain Melog's horse had come from. This was part of the horse's family.

She turned to see Melog dismounting the white stallion, unbuckling its saddle, and removing it and the blankets from its back. With a quick whip from his hand on its hindquarters, the horse turned in the sand and raced back to where the other feral horses were emerging from the sea. It did not immediately run to join the other horses, but instead trotted over to where Cathyn was standing, turning its head sideways from time to time to watch her. Cathyn knew that all-whites were extremely rare. This one was strange, but beautiful. The red mark on its forehead seemed to brighten back to life. She could hear its labored breathing. It seemed anxious about something. It looked from her to Melog and back again. Both the stallion and Tempest exchanged loud huffs. They shook their manes furiously. They were talking to one another. The stallion looked at Melog again, and then turned to look deep into Cathyn's eyes. Those red eyes. It was pawing the sand around them. Cathyn had the distinct feeling that it was trying to tell her something. So many things on this journey had tried to warn her. But it was too late now. She was too far into it to worry. The warrior in her had geared up long ago for whatever danger lay ahead.

Presently the horse broke off and began running down the beach, along the water, in the direction from which she and Melog had just come. It joined up with its other brothers and sisters as they played along the surf. Some ventured up to the hills to graze. Cathyn put her boots back on, grabbed Tempest's reins in her hand, and trotted to catch up with Melog. He had not stopped walking the whole time that Cathyn had had her encounter with the white stallion. She and Tempest reached him after a few moments, and then they slowed to a walk just behind him. She remained on foot. She did not want to be the only one riding.

The sun was still trying to show itself from behind dark storm clouds. It was raining even harder now, but neither traveler seemed to mind. After two or more kilometers of walking, Cathyn broke the silence.

"What can you tell me about those horses?" she yelled above the sound of the waves.

The gray man did not stop walking. Didn't even turn to look at her.

"They're feral!" she continued. "Are they different than the horses we have back home?"

Melog thought about this. "They are more intelligent than the ones you are familiar with!" he answered, also at a yell.

"How so?"

He sighed. He obviously did not want to answer these questions. "They come from a long line of horses that were trained by the royal family. They were the best breed in the country. No other horses could compare to them. They had what we call a mind-connect; they could mentally connect with whomever was riding them and second-guess their masters. This herd that you just saw comes from a field of horses that was on a ship being delivered to…"—he looked over at her—"another place. The ship was trying to negotiate through a storm. It went under, close to shore. The horses rescued themselves and went wild. These are them." He waved at the beach behind them.

"Did you pick the white stallion that you rode to me from these horses?" Cathyn asked.

"Yes." The rain was hitting their faces hard now. "I've ridden that one before. We have...an understanding." His gaze moved out to the ocean.

"You have an appreciation for those horses?" Cathyn asked it more as a statement than a question.

There was a long pause as Melog evidently struggled with this answer. He said nothing. The two travelers fell back into silence.

CHAPTER 10

FORTRESS

It was a long time walking in the sand. The hard rain had not let up. Cathyn could feel a clouded sun on the back of her hood. It was when it had moved well past noon that Cathyn finally looked up and stopped.

Far away from them, sitting out on the water, close to the shoreline, was a giant building. It was perfectly square, a cube, and its walls looked like they were made of the seawater that they were sitting on. Indeed, the entire structure had the appearance of being something that had sprouted up out of the ocean itself. Waves licked along its sides.

"What is this?" Cathyn asked.

"It is our destination!" shouted Captain Melog above the wind and the rain. "It is my home!" he continued after a pause. "It is where I was born!" Here he looked at her. "And it is where you will find your mother!"

Cathyn walked toward her guide and faced him, her back turned to the square building in the water. "This is a blatant trap!" she yelled. She was near tears now out of both anger and an intense feeling that threatened to overwhelm her. The tears mixed on her face with the ocean breeze and the rain. "That's a solid box! If I walk into that…there's no telling what will happen to me! There's no guarantee that my mother is even in there! What makes you think that I should walk in there with you? That could be my prison!"

Melog stared back at her, rain dripping down his nose and mustache. He did not answer, just pushed past her and continued walking toward the building. She knew, though, what the answer was—she would go in. Not to go in would be impossible for her now. She would always wonder. And this is what warriors did anyway, wasn't it? Faced their fears. Besides, how could it be a trap for her? Why would anyone want her, Cathyn? She was just a girl, a warrior's daughter.

With the sounds of waves crashing to her right, and the wind making her hood flap about her head, Cathyn turned to Tempest and put her own cheek up against the horse's cheek. She pointed to a tuft of land farther up the beach, just ahead of the fortress. It was speckled with marsh grass and low shrubs. The horse turned his head as well, as if he understood.

"I want you to go there and graze. I want you to wait for me." She patted his neck. "Can you do that for me?" She paused for the difficult part. "If I don't come out in two days..." She paused again. "I want you to go join the feral horses." She turned and pointed behind them. The horse turned and looked. "They'll take you in. They'll be lucky to have you." She looked into Tempest's eyes. "As I was lucky to have you." She unbuckled the saddle, removed it, the saddle blankets, and her backpack, and tossed them all to the sand. Then she swatted the horse's flank. He ran toward the grassy field. She turned back toward the ocean and approached the structure.

It was enormous. She had thought earlier that it was closer than it was, but now that she had walked a bit, half a kilometer at least, the thing seemed to not be getting any nearer. It was almost as big as the Academy, where she had spent so many years. The perfect fortress—large, square, with no discernable doors or windows. No way in, no way out.

Sea spray struck her face hard and made her sniff. She could see, even from this distance, jutting out from the fortress was a walkway, just as smooth and watery as the object from which it trailed. It was raised out of the water about the full height of an arm.

Trudging through the sand and being whipped by the cold ocean rain, they finally reached the water structure. They stood looking directly at the front of it and its walkway. Without a pause, Melog walked along the path and toward the wall facing them. From nowhere, a double door opened up, and the guide walked in.

Cathyn stood at the edge of the walkway, looking on. The walk was considerable—at least thirty meters to the wall where Melog had vanished. She checked herself, took a deep breath, and tightened her right hand around her longsword. She felt the sinews in her leg ripple along her shin strap. Her mother's armband seemed to hug her muscle, giving her a feeling of reassurance. She walked toward the fortress.

The walkway was slimy, like rock covered with moss. Small waves crashed into the slight bank of it and broke over Cathyn's feet. The water was icy cold. The touch of it crept into her boots. She felt the beginnings of an earache coming on. She sniffled.

Just then, a hand emerged from the water and grabbed her right ankle. At almost the exact moment, another hand grabbed her left ankle. It was impossible for it to be the same creature. It had to be two, one on each side. It was an incredibly vulnerable position to be in; one pull from each hand at the same time would have Cathyn straddling the walkway in a splits position. Next, they would pull her straight down in a move that could easily break the bottom of her spinal column or, if the creatures were strong enough, rip her in half as they swam out in opposite directions.

Cathyn looked down. As she was reaching for her longsword, she noticed that the hands around her ankles were scaly but beautiful, gleaming all colors in the diffused light of the stormy sky. In the next instant, she swung the sword down in a backhanded sweep from behind her to in front of her and cut away the hand on her right ankle. It flopped, fishlike, on the walkway and fell back into the ocean. A deep and startled scream bubbled up from underneath the water.

Without waiting for a reaction from the other hand, she twirled the sword in a backward pass and was now swinging it down and toward her left. Too slow. The remaining hand let go and disappeared into the cold water.

Cathyn waited, sword in hand, for the next attack. It came instantly and without warning. A body, hurling itself through the air, hit her broadside on the right and forced her into the ocean. It was not the side that she had expected; the two-handed beast must have swum underneath the walkway.

She was out of her element now and in the creatures' own territory. If she didn't get out soon, she would be overcome and drowned. She watched as her mother's bow floated to the near bottom of the berm face. The creature that had smashed against her had been flipped forward in the water. It now was doubling back, eyes on her the entire time.

Cathyn saw everything. It was the soldier's responsibility during battle to see everything, sense everything, and make lightning-fast decisions based on what was happening or bound to happen with each passing heartbeat. Now she could see that the creature looked like a waterling. The waterlings that she was familiar with in her world looked just like people, but they lived and breathed in the water. They were a civil and productive race that dealt amicably with the land people. The only other thing different about them were their webbed hands and toes, and hardly noticeable gills on the sides of their necks. This one was more fish than man. Its skin was covered in green and glinting scales, its hands webbed, but its feet were more like flippers. There were very large gills on either side of its neck. It did not seem to have a nose. Large lips opened to reveal sharp teeth that were made for tearing.

She could just make out the faint outline of the creature whose hand she had cut off moments ago swimming away, its mutilated arm tucked closely to its body. The one remaining waterling had disappeared on the other side of a tall and skinny rock structure that had formed eons ago near to the crest. Seaweed floated around the rocks in a caressing motion, almost like long, thin fingers beckoning for her to come to it. At first, Cathyn thought the waterling was hiding. But within moments, it finally revealed itself in the dark of the water world. The creature now had a makeshift spear in its right hand, and it was rushing toward her at tremendous speed. Cathyn could make out its almost black, lidless eyes open wide in order to take in the little bit of light made available underwater.

Paddling her feet to keep herself upright, she switched hands with her sword. She was already feeling the hunger for air, but she knew that this encounter came first.

True to form, the waterling rocketed toward her midsection. Cathyn, however, was an excellent swimmer. She pivoted to the right at the last moment, allowing the creature to bypass without incident. She sliced at its webbed foot as it passed her shoulders. Contact. An ink started to swirl from the wound and spiral toward the surface. The thing wasted no time. It made a backward flip, head over heels, and was now approaching her upside down, spear held directly toward her head. Cathyn arched her back toward the floor of the berm face so that, for a heartbeat, she was riding belly to belly with the creature. Too close to use its spear, the thing grabbed her throat with its free hand. She drove her sword into the waterling's chest. It let out a howl that could be heard even through the thickness of the water, the air bubbling out of its mouth in a torrent. The area surrounding the waterling became inky black. Cathyn grabbed the opportunity to hoist herself back onto the walkway.

She remained there on her stomach, half in the water, half out, coughing and catching her breath.

After ten full gulps of air, she plunged feetfirst back into the water. Looking around quickly for any other waterlings, she saw her mother's bow jammed into the sandy floor, in an almost upright position. She swam to it, grabbed it, and brought it back to the walkway. She would not leave this behind. Breathing hard again, she hoisted herself up and all the way out. She sat there on the magic-made path, panting, cross-legged, eyes searching the water for any swift movement just beneath it. Nothing came. She resheathed her sword and stood up.

The double doors were open again, as if beckoning her. It was dark inside, but she could detect no movement. She strung her mother's bow back onto her shoulder, collected herself, took one last deep breath, and walked in.

CHAPTER 11

THE WHITE WOMAN

She found herself standing in a dark, rounded, tunnel-like hallway. It was at least two heads taller than she was and twice the width of her outstretched arms on either side. Cathyn could hear the sound of moving water roiling all around her. It was the same sound she had heard when she stood behind the waterfall near her house. She moved toward her right and touched the rounded wall of blue. Her hand went through it, cool water separating from the wall and splashing all over it. She moved her hand in a semicircle above her head and to her left. All water, but somehow remaining in place. Remarkable, she thought. Her hunch was correct; someone has magicked the ocean water to serve as the very foundation of this building.

Eventually, the tunnel-hall ended, and she entered an enormous oval-shaped room with one tall wall that wrapped around the entire length of the room. It seemed streaked with subtle vertical striations. There were no windows, but light was coming in from the highest sections of the wall itself. All around the room was a dark blue, like the water that the wall pretended to imitate. But as it stretched far above Cathyn's head, the dark blue webbed into ever-lightening hues that coalesced into an almost white at the very top. Cathyn thought that it must have been made out of some kind of membrane that allowed outside light to shine through, yet was probably strong enough to withstand nature's own elements, as well as any man-made assaults that happened to beset it. Impressive magic.

As her eyes traveled down the height of the room, she noticed a tremendous chandelier-like object, unlike anything that Cathyn had ever seen before, hanging in the air in the exact middle of the room. It hovered on its own, attached to nothing, rotating slowly and radiating a swath of soft white light across everything. It made a sound as it turned, a tinkling, like many small wind chimes shifting together on a porch. It was a shimmering, moving wheel sending lights and shadows dancing everywhere.

Underneath the chandelier was a long table, very thick, made of some sturdy, dark wood. A few plates, complete with utensils and goblets, were set out in front of each of the chairs. Two large blue china pitchers, containing some sort of ice-cold liquid in them, rested on either side of the table, droplets of water running down their sides. A bowl of fruit, and another bowl of bread and cheese, sat opposite one another near the farthest end from Cathyn. She could hear herself dripping water onto the stone floor. It drew attention to the quiet of the awkward moment. A faint mechanical sound could be heard working hard very far away below her.

Melog stood at the end of the table, next to a tall chair. Sitting in the chair was a woman. Almost everything about her was colorless. Her long, straight hair was completely white. Her black robes were decorated with a silver filigree weaving throughout the length of it, from the shoulders to the hem. Her skin was so white as to be almost transparent. Cathyn even thought that she was glowing slightly. Or maybe that was the effect of the bright light reflecting off of her body. She had heard of these types of people before. This woman was an albino. Even sitting, she seemed very tall. Her back was straight, and she was holding a goblet in her right hand.

"Your journey is over, Cathyn Bood. Come and sit," said the white woman. She seemed very relaxed, as if she had just greeted her neighbor to tea.

Cathyn cautiously walked toward the end of the table. There were chairs situated along the length of the table on both sides. Cathyn chose one that was three chairs away from the woman, not too close, but close enough to assess this new opponent. Cathyn did not sit down, but remained standing behind the chair.

Melog stood at an at-ease position next to the white woman. He stared straight ahead, apparently ready to do the woman's bidding at a moment's notice. The chandelier quietly tinkled as it turned.

"Where is my mother?" Cathyn whispered.

The woman took a sip from the goblet. "Please, you are safe now. Your mother is safe as well. And, yes, she is here. We have all the time in the world, Cathyn. Please sit. You *must* let your guard down now. I know you have been in your soldier mode for almost two days. But, please..." The woman gestured with her hand for Cathyn to sit.

Reluctantly, Cathyn pulled out the chair and sat down. She laid her sword on the table next to her. The white woman's voice was friendly and reassuring. It made Cathyn want to trust her. Perhaps this was one of her powers. But Cathyn would not let her guard down. She could, however, play the game, make the woman think that she was relaxed.

The white woman showed no reaction to Cathyn revealing her weapon in so blatant a fashion, but continued sipping at her drink. It was here that Cathyn noticed the woman's face.

It was thin and sallow with sharp, high cheekbones—a beautiful face, really—in its translucent skin. But it was the eyes that were the most interesting. The woman didn't seem to have any pupils. Instead, where one might find some color or darkness in the center of the eye, there was only white. It was a white that Cathyn had never seen in an eye before, not like a cataract, which covers the pupil with a milky film. This was purely white, completely white, as if the pupils had never existed or had been somehow scraped from the roundness of the lens. Around the eyes were tiny scars crisscrossing out like miniature spiderwebs across her cheeks and forehead. This woman was blind.

"I am blind," the woman whispered.

Cathyn stopped breathing. Was the woman reading her mind or just extremely astute at following the natural flow of someone else's thought patterns?

"No, I cannot read minds. I just know what you are looking at now and what you probably are thinking. The fact that you stopped breathing—yes, I can hear even that tiny sound—tells me that I was probably correct, yes?"

"Yes," Cathyn whispered. "You are correct. You followed the direction of my thoughts completely."

The woman drank some more. "Would you like something to drink? Some wine? There's some water on the table next to you."

Cathyn took a small pitcher and poured out a gobletful of water. She put her finger in the liquid and tasted it. No signs of poison. She drank half and put the goblet down. She wiped her mouth with the back of her hand. "Where is my mother?"

"I will take you to her soon. Are you upset?"

What a remarkable question, Cathyn thought. She wouldn't have used that particular word, though. She answered cautiously. "I feel as though there is a game being played here that is not showing me all of its pieces."

The woman smiled. "Well put. There is a game being played here, and not all of the pieces have been shown to you. But they will be shown to you now." She turned her head slowly from one side to the other, as if she was listening closely to something that Cathyn could not hear. "Are you scared?"

Cathyn did not answer right away. Instead she brought all of her inner strength to bear in an effort to compose herself. She did not want to show this white woman any hint of fear, but she also knew that she had to be honest, completely honest. This woman would know if Cathyn was hiding anything. This was a test of wills. Cathyn must become not scared. "A warrior knows how to deal with fear. I can work around fear. My mother taught me that."

"I'm sure she did. The great Kaal Bood, commander of the Second Color Militia. She's...legendary," the woman sighed.

"You say that almost with disgust," Cathyn hissed. "She is the great Kaal Bood. She is a great commander."

The woman paused to take this in. She seemed to be looking for an answer. "Yes...well...she's here now, at my disposal, no longer commanding anything and no longer...so great."

This gave Cathyn a turn. It did not sound good. It was time to play the offensive.

"You are Lady Abathet," Cathyn whispered.

The woman paused, turned her scarred, but beautiful face straight on Cathyn. "Lady Abathet is dead."

CHAPTER 12
THE BATTLE OF THE SUNS

This was more information than Cathyn could take in. Her entire journey seemed fraught with surprises, and she had allowed herself to be caught off guard too often. It was one of the warrior's skills to be able to accept the unexpected instantly and then deal with it, adapt to it. But here she was being caught off guard once again.

The white woman seemed to enjoy drawing out the moment. She let the pause work on Cathyn. "I am her sister, Silyaac," she answered finally. She could hear Cathyn working on her breathing in an effort to control herself. "Lady Abathet was killed in a... great...great battle," continued Silyaac quietly. "The greatest battle of our time."

"The Battle of the Suns," Cathyn whispered. "My mother told me about it. We learned about it at the Academy." She looked at the table, trying to remember.

"It took place in the Orington Fields, two hundred kilometers from our home."

"It took place here…even farther from your home." Silyaac turned her head. "Farther, and yet closer than you think, I suspect."

Yes, closer than Cathyn thought. Because here she was, within an easy day-and-half ride, on an ocean that was not supposed to exist.

"The Battle of the Suns," Silyaac continued. "Your mother, Kaal Bood, and her militia were there, of course, as were Lady Abathet and her army. The royal family, my family, looked on from a hill not far from where the battle took place." Silyaac seemed to be looking into her own blindness, reliving the event. "The two armies were lined up facing one another. It was the pivotal skirmish of the battle. It would, we believed at the time, decide the war."

"War?" Cathyn breathed.

"Yes, war. Your mother never told you? What did you think this battle was all about?"

"She said that they were repelling an invading force."

"Ah." Silyaac smiled. "And did she tell you where this 'invading force' came from?"

"She said they were from the other side of the Selton Mountains."

"Did she tell you that the invading force…was actually them?"

Cathyn was speechless.

The white woman continued. "The Battle of the Suns was merely the last battle of a great war that has been going on for some time. It is a war between two worlds, yours and mine. Lady Abathet was ruler here in this world. She'd been so all of her adult life. For generations the royal family had overseen all that goes on here, and for all of that time, it had been amassing power, getting stronger. And then it all fell to Lady Abathet.

"Out of all the royal family, only she and myself were sorceresses. There had been others with powers in the past, but none in quite some time. Something ran through our blood that seemed diluted in all of our recent ancestors' veins. Perhaps it was our albinism." She paused. "Even as a child, my sister exhibited almost complete control over natural things. Just by the merest glance or gesture, she could move any object or, by speaking the ancient language, transform it into something else. That is true magic. But my magic was different, not as powerful. And besides, I was the younger sister. It was she who was in power. It was her confidence and leadership that was unquestionable. And rightly so. She was a true leader.

"And so it was decided that the time was right for a rent to be opened between the two worlds, and a surprise attack was to be mounted by Lady Abathet and her army. If successful, then the royal family would rule over the two known worlds. All who still lived would swear allegiance to the royal family...to us. As it should be."

"But it wasn't a surprise," Cathyn guessed.

"No. Somehow the attack was known, and word spread quickly to your mother and her Second Color Militia. They found their own way here. How, we do not know. But they met at the valley just on this side of the tear and challenged Lady Abathet's plans of annex. Even with surprise no longer an aspect of the attack, Lady Abathet was confident of victory. After all, she was a sorceress. Magic was her ally. And then, just as the trumpets sounded the charge and both armies began their swift descents into the valley, the air was rocked with explosions."

"Explosions?" Cathyn gasped. "What kind of weapons—"

But Silyaac did not let Cathyn finish. "Not weapons...magic. Not the royal magic of me and my sister. Not the magic that coursed through the bodies of the royal families. This was an unknown magic, something we had never seen before. A great warping of the elements that burned us and crushed us all like small things."

Here, Silyaac took a deep breath. "Within moments of the explosions, there were burning, searing globes moving through the valley, rolling over our army. Some hovered, like blazing suns laying waste to already dead planets. Others ran along the ground, smashing and burning everything in their paths. There wasn't even a chance to retreat. They were everywhere, even rolling in from behind. These suns, these glowing fireballs, moved as if with minds of their own, plowing through our soldiers, blasting them to nothingness in an instant. Our soldiers..." She paused, remembering. "They would spark, flare up like matches, and then disappear, just wisps of smoke left lingering in the air. And the sounds..." Silyaac sighed, looking down. "I can still hear them, the sounds of the soldiers disappearing and the roiling suns exploding, that low hum as they tore through our land and their brave bodies." She stood now, holding on to the rim of the table, facing the entrance to the hall.

"Lady Abathet did not survive. She led the charge and so was one of the first to ride into the fires." She turned in the direction of Cathyn. "A true leader. See? I told you so." She dropped her head. "Her destiny, I suppose." She took a deep breath, adjusted her robe. "But I was watching from the hill as one of the suns veered off suddenly and came racing toward me. I remember being knocked down by someone, and then an intense heat on my face. The sky seemed to become white, and I heard a tiny, far-off sound, a crackling sound, as if someone were cooking meat on a spit. My eyes. And then I saw my world burst into colors and explode away. It was the last thing I was ever to see."

Silyaac turned from the table and walked to Cathyn's chair. She stood behind it. She walked confidently, as if she could see everything around her.

Cathyn did not turn around in her direction, showing no fear. It was a ruse. She remained tense. Listening.

"And so some of us survived...though at what price, I ask myself. The Second Color Militia retreated back to your world, and the tear closed, leaving us to tend to our wounded and dying. There was a funeral for my sister and the others who served her, although no bodies were ever found of that first vanguard that rode toward the suns. I, meanwhile, was brought here to our closest outpost to recover." She looked up past Cathyn, over to where Melog was standing. "Captain Melog was assigned to serve me." She smiled. "And he's served me well. He's been my right-hand man in all things." There was no reaction from the guard. "And so we've been here for all this time...waiting."

"Waiting for what?" Cathyn asked.

Silyaac bent down close to Cathyn behind her. Cathyn could feel the white woman's breath on her neck. "Do you know what my powers are?" she whispered.

Cathyn answered by doing nothing, waiting for the answer to surely come.

"I am a shape-changer. Can you imagine that? A blind shape-changer? Do you know that I can change my body into anything? A snake, a chair, another person…" She touched Cathyn's hand. "The ghostly image of a woman, a warrior, calling out for help across the void." She smiled.

Cathyn pulled her hand away. "You!" She turned toward the white woman. "It wasn't my mother at all. It was you! You were the image I saw in the window!"

Silyaac walked back toward her chair. "I had to get you here somehow. I had to set the bait. It was the one image that you couldn't resist."

Cathyn looked at Melog. "It was a trick. You lied to me and guided me right into it. What is your stake in all of this?"

"First of all," Melog began, "I did not lie. Your mother is here, and I've brought you to her. Secondly, my stake in this? I have no stake in anything. I've served the entire run of the royal family for as long as time remembers. I have seen the ages come and go, and I have been there at every change of order to assist my king or queen or next-in-line as best I can."

"How is that possible? How could you have lived so long?"

Melog's expression did not change. His eyes remained cold, his head tilted slightly. "I am an inanimate. An object brought to life by the old magic, the magic that began all of this." His hand motioned to the room. He let the meaning of his words sink in. "I am immortal. I cannot die."

"So...what were you before...a statue that someone sculpted out of clay...that someone brought to life?"

There was a silence between them now that stretched to fill the large room. Melog, looking straight at Cathyn, seemed to move his face into subtle contortions, as if truly figuring out how best to answer her.

"I do not speak of that time," he whispered. "There is no time before life."

"Take me to my mother!" Cathyn slammed her hand on the table.

Silyaac slowly brought her arms back and stretched. "The great Kaal Bood has been here for some time now, captured in a state of cold sleep."

"What is cold sleep?" asked Cathyn.

"She does not move. She does not speak. She does not eat. Yet she lives and breathes. I do not think she ages. She'll appreciate that when she wakes," she added as an aside. "If the trance were not broken, I do believe that she'd live forever...like my guardian here, Captain Melog. But come with me. I will break the spell at long last and wake her for you. We all need to talk."

"Wait." Cathyn stood up. "What are you after? Why am I here with my mother?"

But the sorceress was already walking out of the room at a clipped pace. Cathyn grabbed her sword from the table and walked quickly to keep up, Melog close behind.

"Sheathe your sword, Cathyn Bood!" Silyaac yelled from ahead. "It won't serve you here."

Reluctantly, she did.

Cathyn entered a winding, curving hallway, this one seemingly made of stone. She waited for Melog to pass her and take the lead. She followed him down two other hallways and finally into a room that glowed so brightly, Cathyn had to shield her eyes with her hand. A humming noise filled the room. After her eyes adjusted, she could see, in the center of the room, a glowing body, hovering above the floor, straight out in a prone position. It was Cathyn's mother. Silyaac stood next to her.

"What are you doing to her?" asked Cathyn.

"I'm not doing anything to her," answered Silyaac. "I told you, she's in a state of cold sleep until we are in a position to negotiate." She said this without turning her head toward Cathyn, while looking straight at Cathyn's mother, as if she could really see through her dead eyes.

"What do you mean 'negotiate'?"

Silyaac sighed and walked toward Cathyn's mother. She bent low and walked under her, then, from behind the floating body, passed her hands over top and around it like a magician would do on a stage. It was obvious she felt a sense of pride in her handiwork.

"Well…she's my bargaining chip. Don't you know anything about strategy? What did they teach you at the Academy?"

"I learned strategy," Cathyn answered tersely. "I just don't know what kind of strategy you have in mind. Why do you need both of us?"

Still moving her hands slowly around the body of Cathyn's mother, Silyaac, without actually touching her, somehow turned the figure so that it was upright and facing forward. The energy field that danced around Kaal Bood dissipated. Silyaac placed her fingers on Cathyn's mother's eyes and then moved them away. The eyes opened.

"Mother!" Cathyn cried.

The woman warrior was tall, almost as tall as Captain Melog. She was lean and muscular. Her hair was cut short and was black, like her daughter's, but sported a streak of white that ran through the middle of her hairline. Her eyes were large and as green as Cathyn's, her face handsome and warm. Kaal Bood sighed and moved her head slowly from side to side, and around, like an athlete getting the kinks out of her neck and shoulders. She looked over at her daughter standing next to Silyaac. "I was afraid of this. How are you, my darling?"

Cathyn ran forward and threw her arms around her mother's neck. She hugged her tight. "I'm fine. I'm fine," she whispered. "Everyone thought you were dead, but I knew that you weren't," she sobbed. "Something inside of me told me that you weren't."

"Silyaac," Kaal Bood announced, "you've entered into a dangerous level by bringing my daughter here. You have no idea what you're dealing with now. Hurt her, and I swear your body will follow your dead eyes."

"Oh, you're so dramatic, Kaal," Silyaac responded. "You were always such a showy warrior. The fact is, it's you who doesn't know what she's dealing with." She began walking, motioning for Cathyn and her mother to follow her. "In case you haven't noticed, you're both my prisoners, in my territory and in my power. Neither of you could get out of my fortress alive. And now that you're both here, you have each other to watch out for, a considerable liability, don't you agree? Which, interestingly enough, brings me to our negotiations. But I think we'd better sit for this."

They followed Silyaac out of the room, Cathyn and her mother walking arm in arm. The four of them took another turn in the winding, round hallway, walking into a smaller, darker room with a fire and a couch and a medium-sized rectangular table with chairs. Again, there were bowls of fruit and plates of bread and cheese, along with tall glasses of wine and water, on the table. Captain Melog stood nearby against a wall that was adorned with a colorful tapestry. An army on the tapestry fended off a herd of beasts in a densely packed forest. It was a bloody event. The guide's gray figure stood out against the garish scene.

"Please…sit," said Silyaac as she pulled up a chair. "You may as well eat. We all have to eat." She shot a blind glance at Melog.

Kaal Bood sat down next to Silyaac. Cathyn sat across from her mother. "I have no hunger, Silyaac. Your spell has slowed down all of my bodily functions. My daughter will eat, however." She looked across at Cathyn and nodded. "Please eat. You'll need your strength," she whispered.

Cathyn understood. Escaping from Silyaac's fortress was going to be mostly up to her. Any good warrior knew that you needed to take sleep and food when you could find them. The battles would eventually come. She reached for the fruit and bread.

"So, talk to us, Silyaac," said Kaal Bood directly. "What do you want? My armies won't surrender to you just because you have me and my daughter as prisoners. It would be foolhardy and unwise. They are extremely loyal, but they're not stupid. I'm afraid they consider us, at this point, merely spoils of war."

Silyaac had also started eating. She took a sip of wine to wash it down. "Oh, nothing so grand as all of that, Kaal. I just want your eyes," she whispered.

CHAPTER 13

THE EYES OF
THE SORCERESS

"My eyes!" laughed Kaal Bood. "Are you insane? Just because you went and got your own eyes blasted out in battle! It's the consequence of war, Silyaac. Learn to live with it."

"But that's just it, Kaal," sighed the sorceress. She dropped her lips into a slight pout. "I don't want to learn to live with it. A sorceress is only as good as what she can see to cast a spell on, especially a shape-changer. Being blind limits my powers considerably, and, well, you know, we can't have that. And now, having you both here gives me my best chance at seeing again."

"How so?" hissed the warrior woman.

"Oh, come now, Commander. Surely you know where I'm going with this. Or is it that you just need to hear me say it?" Silyaac smiled and lifted her head as if she were smelling something in the air. She actually winked at her old foe. "That's it, isn't it? You don't want to be responsible for giving voice to your own fears. If you say it, it will happen. And so, being the bad one, I am forced to say it. All right, then…I'll say it. I want one of your pair of eyes. Either yours or your daughter's, I don't much care which. If you won't give me yours, then I will be forced to kill your lovely daughter here. Or maybe your daughter will give me hers, and then I won't be forced to kill you. One way or another, one of you is going to willingly turn over her eyes…for me."

"Why must we willingly give them to you?" barked Cathyn. "Why don't you just take them?"

Silyaac did not answer. She paused to sip her wine.

"She can't take them," answered her mother, her eyes still on the face of her enemy. "It's part of the magic that will make it work. The eyes must be given over willingly. I've only heard of something like this once before.

"There was a man in the mountains who gave over his heart to a young boy who was dying. He was also a sorcerer, and he made the transfer effortlessly and painlessly. The boy lived a good long life after that. Even became a warrior in one of our armies. He saved the lives of many men and women. See how well graciousness and generosity play out?" She paused to let Silyaac get the point.

"The sorcerer lived only one other day. He knew that his time was short, so he meditated and did good works. And then he died because he no longer had a heart inside of his body to move his blood. But that is not what is happening here. That was an act of goodness, of light. This, here, is an act of darkness."

"Call it what you like, Kaal." The blind sorceress took over. "Being blind is darkness. I would even go as far as to say that it is not unlike death." She paused and whispered, "No, it's like walking alongside death. I can sense the world around me, but I cannot see it. My internal powers are hushed, as if a great blanket has been put over them. There's a part of me that cannot actually be in this world!"

At this, Silyaac stood up. Sighing, she took a moment to regain her composure. "It is a necessary step that will bring my powers back to full potential. And it is those powers that will bring me back to the rightful reign of this country that is now mine, and the eventual annexation of yours."

Cathyn had not stopped watching Silyaac. "How did you mimic my mother? How did you look and sound like her if you couldn't see her?"

"That was easy. My senses of touch and hearing are intact. In fact, I believe they're enhanced. Your mother was here as my prisoner. I had only to touch her face, feel the outline of her body to get the imitation just right. Her voice was stored away in my memory. But I can't do that in all instances. I don't always have the luxury of having my enemies here with me so that I may study them. No, I need to see in order to fully assume a shape. I need to see in order to conquer."

Silyaac closed her hand into a fist. She walked over to the open doorway leading down the tunnel hallways. "So…I'll leave you two to think it over. Decide who will relinquish their eyes so that we can put an end to this and I can send you two back home. I'll even allow my captain to guide you back over to the other side. You'll be no threat to me…after the fact. In the meantime, Melog will take you back to the room where Kaal was suspended and stand guard to make sure no one goes anywhere prematurely. That door that you first entered"—she pointed in the direction of the first room—"is now sealed. I'll give you until tonight to decide. We'll perform the exchange in the morning. If you decide not to grant my wish, then I'll kill you both. Proof that I have killed the great Kaal Bood and her warrior daughter will be another grand bargaining chip for future negotiations with someone else. Either way, I win." Silyaac smiled and began to walk away, turned, and stopped. "But I would so… appreciate it if you would act in accordance with my plans. The magic only works when what you have is relinquished willingly. And the darkness…it wears on me." She walked out of the sitting room, the fabric in her cloak then rustling down the hallway.

Melog turned to Cathyn. He put out his hands. Cathyn knew what he wanted. It was difficult for her to respond. She pulled her mother's bow and quiver of arrows off of her shoulder and put them in his black-gloved hands. She unbuckled the scabbard that held her longsword and gave that to him. She stopped at this point, hoping that the dark guard had forgotten. He hadn't. His hands were still beckoning. She sighed and unstrapped her shin sheath and knife and turned those over as well. Melog took his bounty and walked out of the room.

Cathyn turned back to her mother. "I am going to let her take my eyes," she stated in an even tone. Her mind was made up. "You are the greatest warrior our country has ever had. You are a leader. You must be ready to gather our armies to fight Silyaac once she is back in power."

"Is this my daughter talking, or another great warrior willing to give her life for the cause?" Her mother smiled. "I have raised a good soldier. You have grown up so much, and I am so proud of you." She touched her daughter's face. "But, no…she will not get my daughter's eyes. She will get mine, and she knows this. Silyaac has outmaneuvered us, I think."

"It's all my fault. I fell right into her trap, coming along with Melog to try and find you. She led me like a farmer leads his oxen."

Kaal Bood was quiet at this. "We must do what soldiers do, my darling. If we both fight, we both may die, and I cannot allow that to happen to you. You are my flesh. You are all I have. We must lose this battle in order to regroup and fight another day."

There was a pause in the conversation. Melog had reentered the room. "Can I get you anything, Commander Bood?"

"Don't even talk to us," hissed Cathyn. "You brought me here. You can do nothing for us now."

"I am…bound to Lady Silyaac. It is in her service that I have been placed. I can do nothing else. And I serve her well."

"You serve darkness well," Cathyn whispered, and spit on the ground. She motioned for her mother to follow her. They walked out of the small sitting room and down the tunnel from where they had come. They talked as they walked, Melog following behind.

"Mother, how did Silyaac get you here? The last I heard, you had been summoned to battle. Your soldiers who came back, they said that they saw you…"

"Yes…What did they say that they saw?" Kaal Bood seemed concerned.

"They say they saw you struck by something, a bolt of lightning, and then you were engulfed in flames. They said all that was left of your body were ashes. They said the battle had ended at that moment, that the warriors they had been summoned to fight had disappeared. They figured that it was all just a trick to get you into a position to assassinate you." Another thought struck Cathyn. "I think Bark saw the whole thing. He didn't say you were killed. He said that you were taken."

Kaal Bood arched her eyebrows and smiled. "Ah, yes. Bark. Leave it to him to see what is really happening around us all." Her smile vanished. "To be honest, I don't remember much of what happened. I do remember the battle, a small skirmish between a ragtag band of strangely outfitted fighters and thirty of our best soldiers, on our side of the world this time. Obviously, Silyaac must have allies amongst our own soldiers and diplomats." She looked directly at Cathyn. "Something we'll have to address when we return."

"Traitors," Cathyn hissed.

"There are always traitors, my darling."

Cathyn shook her head. She was still too trusting.

"Anyway," the mother warrior continued, "the fight was going well, none lost on our side. Three or four of hers were slain... when I heard a high-pitched hum above me. And then everything went white... and silent. And then I remember seeing Silyaac's figure approaching me in the darkness. She said something to me. I remember talking to her, but about what, I don't know. I saw us approaching this fortress on the water. I recall that main room and some of the hallways as if in a mist." She paused and looked again at her daughter. "And then I woke up and saw you." Kaal Bood smiled at her daughter. "How long have I been missing?"

"Almost six months," Cathyn whispered. "Why did she wait so long?"

Kaal Bood thought about this. "She must have been working on how to get into our world. If Captain Melog was the one who brought you to her, perhaps she has only been able to figure out how to get him through the portal. That is something to think about."

"So...you've known of this other world."

"Yes. For some time now. All of the battles that I've told you about, all of the skirmishes and the deaths and the victories, have been about us holding on to and protecting our world from an invasion from the forces of this world. At first it was a powerful king named Jans. And then it was his daughter, Abathet. And now it seems it is Silyaac."

They had come to the doorway of the chamber where Kaal Bood had been awakened from her cold sleep. Cathyn looked over her shoulder. Captain Melog was still walking toward them from the far end of the tunnel. They stepped into the room.

"Mother, we must find a way to escape," Cathyn whispered. "Silyaac cannot get your eyes. It would be a victory for her that we cannot afford."

They heard Captain Melog locking the door behind them. It had the sound of something final.

"I agree, young warrior." Kaal Bood smiled. "And I'm ready to implement any suggestions you might have. The ox, this time, is leading the farmer, I think?" She looked around the small stone room. "Well, I have apparently been sleeping for a long time. I'm not sleepy in the least. How about you?"

"Nor I," Cathyn answered. "We will stay up and work out a plan. This sorceress will not win. She has two warrior women together in this room. That's a dangerous situation."

"Hmmm. For her or for us?"

It made Cathyn smile.

Kaal Bood looked intensely at her daughter. She closed her eyes and breathed slowly three times. Cathyn knew that she was doing the meditation breaths in order to clear her mind. She opened her eyes and looked at her daughter. "What is the first thing to do when assessing a situation?"

"Discover what you already know," Cathyn repeated from her lessons at the Academy. "What do you know about this place, Mother?"

Kaal Bood thought back. "When I was captured, I saw only two faces of this cube. But there were no windows or doorways visible on any of them. I suspect that Silyaac has magicked her entrances and exits so that only she controls who comes and who goes. At this point, this fortress of hers may well be a solid cube with doorways opened only to those she wishes to enter or exit, and only when she's ready to open them."

"And I saw light coming through the walls in the main entrance," Cathyn added. "Has she made them so that they are solid, but able to bring in sunlight?"

"Very possibly…and not only sunlight. When I was captured, it was night. And yet some kind of light was emanating from the walls." She sighed. "I do not think there are any means of escape, my darling."

"What else do you remember before Silyaac put you in that sleep state?"

"I remember that she talked to me for a bit, in the main hall, just as she did the two of us. I was still in that half-asleep, half-awake state. Then she had Captain Melog walk me down here to this room. I was only conscious for about an hour or so after that, and then Silyaac came down here and talked to me for a bit more. I remember trying to reach for my sword to fight back against her, but I could not raise my arms. My whole body seemed to be paralyzed. Then it all went dark after that. I imagine that's when she put that sleeping spell on me."

"Did you see anything in the hallway tunnel while you were walking down here to this chamber?"

Kaal Bood closed her eyes again. "I do recall thinking how odd it was that the tunnels and the rooms were round inside of a cubical structure. I remember how dirty the tunnels seemed to me, not a place fitting a sorceress with the powers that Silyaac boasts of having. Maybe that owes to her blindness because she can't see all of her surroundings. And I remember that I could hear machines of some kind working far away." She opened her eyes. "She must have other people here in this manse, working those machines. They must be somewhere!" she exclaimed. "Silyaac cannot survive here alone with just Melog to look after her, especially when he's gone. Her sorcery is shape-changing, not manipulating objects in space and time like her sister. She needs to have others working for her."

"You're right." Cathyn looked around the room. "Where are they?" And then she looked at her feet on the floor. Below them, the gentle huffing and puffing of the faraway machines.

Just then they heard a scratching sound nearby, behind Kaal Bood. Turning, they saw a verminlike creature dripping water and scurrying alongside the far wall. It disappeared into a crack at the base. They looked at one another.

"Water rats," Kaal whispered. "They've come here for the food. If they can get in..." She looked at her daughter.

"We can get out."

CHAPTER 14
A CRACKLING SOUND

There were two water rats, one inching its way along the far wall, and another zigzagging between the chair and the table legs. Cathyn and Kaal Bood watched silently. They had become statues, as any good soldier could do at a moment's notice. They were collecting information now and needed to be perfectly silent, invisible, so as not to disturb the vermins' movements. They watched until the one under the table had found food, possibly a scrap of bread. It held it in its jaws for a few seconds, then scurried over to the back wall to join its companion. Together they skittered along the curve of the wall for about five meters, where they disappeared into the floor. The warriors moved over toward it.

Cathyn ran her hands along the floor. "There's a small hole here." She looked up at her mother. "And I feel air."

Kaal Bood surveyed the room, looking up at the ceiling. "These are round rooms inside a cube. Mathematics says that there must be some space in between."

"Yes, but this is a magic place. Do mathematics have a place in magic?"

Kaal Bood looked at her daughter and smiled. "I've always thought that mathematics is a part of magic, in a way." She turned back toward the water rats. "Or maybe it's the other way around."

Cathyn stuck four of her fingers into the hole and pulled. Nothing came up. She looked around the room. "Mother, help me get a leg off that chair."

Kaal Bood turned the chair on its side. She brought the back of her elbow down on it and one of the highest legs snapped off. Catching it with her hand so that Melog would not hear it fall, she handed it to her daughter. Cathyn took the small end of the leg and fitted it into the hole. It was sticking out now as an angled lever. She put her foot up on the high side and pushed down. A flagstone pried up as the lever moved toward the floor. She remained standing on it while Kaal Bood worked at the flagstone with her hands. After about a minute, the flagstone was inched aside, revealing a good-sized hole leading down to a space below. The warriors looked down into the newly formed opening.

There was a second floor just an arm's length below the hole. Cathyn reached down and quietly pried up two large pieces of wood. They could see another room.

This room was very large, three times the height of the one that they were in, and possibly as long and as wide as an entire part of the hallway and the cells that were attached to it. There was a small amount of light coming from the room, and there were sounds, like machines running and...

"Voices," whispered Kaal Bood.

Cathyn listened closer. There were people talking down there. She couldn't see them, but she could hear them. They were far away, but they were talking loudly to be heard over the sounds of the machinery. Her eyes adjusted to the room's light. From what she could see, the machines took up most of the space of the room. They were enormous, great, hulking iron boxes with long tubes of different sizes running out of them. Smaller boxes were camped next to the larger ones—control boxes of some kind, Cathyn thought. One of the larger machines was directly under their hole.

"Mother, I think if I can squeeze through these holes, I could land on the top of that one machine there."

"Then what, my darling? We'll be separated. Silyaac will use me as bait again to get you to return."

"We can't stay here in this room," Cathyn reasoned. "She's got us both all rolled up into one neat package.

If we separate, we can try to sabotage this fortress." She drew herself away from the hole. "But I agree, we can't stay here in this room. We both have got to get out."

"I don't think I can fit through that hole." Kaal Bood smiled. "That is a daughter-sized hole."

"Well, then, let's make it a family-sized hole!" Cathyn exclaimed.

A crackling sound pierced their reverie and made them both jump. They turned back toward the center of the room.

The crackling was coming from another curve in one of the walls that connected to the room next to theirs. As they watched, the wall shimmered in three places, dissolved, then reformed again. A shimmering haze hung in the air, making it difficult to see that part of the wall again.

Cathyn stood up. She knew this effect. She had seen it before. She watched as the shimmering haze approached her.

Kaal Bood walked toward Cathyn, chair leg in hand, ready to beat it off.

"It's all right, Mother. I think help has arrived." She offered her arm in the direction of the shimmer, much as a dancer might offer her arm to a dance partner. The haze surrounded Cathyn's arm, camouflaged it, turning it into a pulsating cloud of light. Then there was a spark, and a man with a bushy beard was holding Cathyn's arm.

"Missy," the man whispered.

"Kettle. I knew it was you. Is this Pitts and Gamliggy?" Cathyn asked, nodding in the direction of the other two figures. Cathyn held out her other arm. Another cloud of light encircled it, sparked, and snapped into the figure of a man.

"Gamliggy at your service, me lady."

"Mother, these are my friends. They're...lightning men. Let the last one touch your arm."

Kaal Bood did as her daughter asked. Within seconds Pitts was standing alongside her.

"Is this your mother, then?" asked Pitts.

"It is. Gentlemen, this is Kaal Bood," answered Cathyn.

"Oh, we've heard of the great Kaal Bood," whispered Kettle. "Indeed we have." He faced Cathyn's mother. "Sandamin Kettle, Your Majesty. These are me mates, Gamliggy and Pitts. We're prospectors. Met your daughter just yesterday up in Abathet Woods. She was kind enough to lend us her...arms...so's that we could get solid for a bit. Awfully nice of your daughter, Commander."

"Kettle, how did you...I thought..." Cathyn began.

"So did we, missy. So did we. Remember what that Lady Abathet told us? We was sure that we was going to explode...or somethin' worse once we set foot outside the woods."

"What happened?"

"Tell her, Kettle," urged Gamliggy. "It's a brave story."

"Well," Kettle began, "we was standin' there at the edge of the woods watchin' you and that…guide of yours ride on away, and we gots to thinkin' and talkin'. One thing about bein' cursed all together like that is that it gives yous time to think and talk."

"Company's getting a little stale, though," whispered Gamliggy.

Kettle harrumphed. "Anyways, we're standin' there thinkin' and talkin' and comin' up with how much it's a shame that you've gots to continue on this search with that there dark soldier at your side, and how you're walkin' into danger for sure, and so we just decided to follow and see what happened."

"Kettle, that was a dangerous thing to do," whispered Cathyn.

Kettle blushed. "Aw, missy. We been cursed in them woods so long, it was time to take a few chances. What kind of men would we be if we didn't? I wouldn't be able to look at meself in the mirror."

"We ain't got a mirror, Kettle," added Gamliggy.

"That's not the point. The point is we had to do somethin'. So I looks at these two rascals, and they looks at me, and what do you know, we all links arms together and starts to walk toward the edge. It took us exactly seven steps to make it to where the woods stopped, and I don't mind sayin', I took each step like it was going to be me last."

"You know, mum, we could have blown up like swamp gas," whispered Pitts. "But we figures, if we're gonna go, we're gonna go together."

"So, what happened?" asked Cathyn.

"Well…that's just it, isn't it? Nothin' happened. We stepped out of them woods, into that little open field just outside the edge there, and…nothin'. I looks at Pitts. Pitts looks at Gamliggy—"

"And we laughs like monkeys, mum. We laugh just like monkeys." Pitts smiled.

"You never heard such laughin'," added Gamliggy. "We falls down we was laughin' so hard, didn't we, Kettle?"

"We did, just like we was kids skipping school." A long grin played across Kettle's face.

"We never went to school," reminded Gamliggy.

Kettle rolled his eyes. But then he settled into a more serious expression. "That's when we knew we'd been duped by that Lady Abathet. All them years, stuck in them woods by a trick. All them years we could of left and maybe found someone to help get us back to normal." He looked straight at Cathyn. "But we thinks it was you, missy, what gives us the reason to calls her bluff. You gives us the courage to go and do it."

"And here we are." Gamliggy announced.

"It weren't difficult to follow you, mum," added Pitts, "what with us bein' old prospectors and such."

"Well, I think you're the bravest men I've ever met," sighed Cathyn.

The three lightning men looked around at one another, smiles on their faces.

It was Kettle who refocused them. "But now we've got a new problem. We've gotten out of the frying pan, but now I'd say we're in the fire for sure."

"I guess the next step is to get off the stove," said Pitts.

"Are we talkin' about cooking?" asked Gamliggy.

"No, sir," corrected Kettle. "We're talkin' about rescuin'."

CHAPTER 15

GETTING OFF THE STOVE

"That's it!" exclaimed Cathyn.

"Did Pitts come up with an idea?" asked Gamliggy. He looked at Pitts. The plump lightning man smiled and looked like he was blushing.

"A brilliant idea." Cathyn smiled. "It's the idiom he used."

Gamliggy looked sour. "Awww now, mum. There's no need to start callin' names now."

"No—we'll attack the stove," she clarified.

"The stove?" repeated Kaal Bood.

"Well, not the stove exactly, but…the power source." She turned to Kettle. "The basic construction of this fortress is magic. But the creators couldn't maintain it with magic. I think they installed some kind of power source for some of it. And I think it's right below us."

Kaal Bood looked above her at the bright glow from the ceiling. "Yes—see? She doesn't use torches or oil to light this place. It's something that we have yet to discover. Good catch, my darling."

"And there's some kind of air-pumping system running that allows the air to move back and forth through these...grids," Cathyn continued. She pointed to a grate at the top of one of the walls. "Probably brings in outside air as well, seeing as there are no windows."

Cathyn's mother gave her an approving look. They realized now that there was, indeed, the faint sound of air moving throughout the room.

"And I know what you can do," Cathyn said, turning to Kettle. "First off, you've got to find our weapons. You can pass through these walls like they aren't even here."

"Well, that's all well and good, missy, but what'll we do when we finds them?" asked Kettle. "We can't pick them up. Our hands will just pass right through them."

"That's all right. Just come back and report to us where they are. We'll find a way later to go back with you to get them. It'll save us time if we don't have to go look for them ourselves. I'll work on the power system." Cathyn looked at the lightning men attached to her arm. "I'll need one of you to go with me."

The three prospectors looked at one another. "I'll go with you, mum," piped up Pitts. "I'm the best at fixin' broken things."

"And breakin' fixed things," Gamliggy whispered to Kettle.

Pitts ignored his friend's remark. "And it'd be better for Kettle to be in charge of the weapons search."

"I agree," said Kettle. "Gamliggy and me can finds them weapons for you."

"It'd probably be best if the two of you took it one room at a time," suggested Kaal Bood. "Cover the first floor completely, room by room. If you haven't found them, move on to the second floor. I'm not even sure how many floors are in this fortress."

"We'll cover them all, ma'am," said Kettle. "If the weapons are here, we'll find them. And fast-like."

"Yeah, we can be mighty fast when we wants to," added Gamliggy with his eyes large and excited.

Cathyn looked at the door leading out to the hallway. "We haven't got much time. Captain Melog is standing guard just down the hall. He could stick his head back in here at any moment to check on us."

Kettle smiled. "I think Gamliggy and me'll give the old Captain a bit of a scare before we goes abouts our business. Keep him busy for a while."

"Excellent. Right. Mother, you wait here for Kettle and Gamliggy to return with news of their search. Pitts and I will go down to the lower level and try to destroy as many of those power sources as we can. As soon as you can, get out and get those weapons. It may mean the three of you taking on Melog by yourselves.

"And be careful. This is not Lady Abathet we're dealing with here. This is her sister, Silyaac. She's blind, but she's deadly dangerous."

Cathyn looked around at the group of them. "Everyone ready?"

They nodded.

"Then let's make some noise."

The lightning men released their grips on Cathyn's and Kaal Bood's arms and disappeared into the air. The women warriors could hear the now-familiar crackling sounds as Kettle and Gamliggy flashed through the wall. Cathyn bent down and sat on the edge of the holes in the two floors, dangling her legs into the air of the space between the rooms below. She could hear Pitts vibrating behind her. She pushed herself off, went through the holes, and, catlike, grabbed on to the edge of the top of the machine room ceiling with her hands. Three good swings back and forth gave her the momentum and the arc that she needed. She let go, flew through the air, and landed on top of one of the machines with a *womp*. A light pop just behind her told her that Pitts had landed as well.

He touched her arm, turned solid for just a moment, and whispered, "Don't think I coulda got through that little hole in me solid form, don'tcha know." He patted his large belly and reenergized.

Cathyn smiled, but remained crouched, listening around her. No voices or reactions from the lower-level workers to their landings. Cathyn, again, grabbed on to the edge of the machine, dangled, and dropped to the ground. Pitts, shimmering just above her, was there, and then he was suddenly beside her, an effect of his hyperspeed mode. She held up her hand, palm open, fingers pointing straight up, as the soldier's silent sign for "wait."

Now that they were on the floor, Cathyn scanned the area, taking in as much detail as she could as quickly as possible.

Machines lined all four walls of the room. A few were in the middle, like the one that she and Pitts had dropped onto. Steam was huffing and puffing out of them from various sections near the floor. A rancid green liquid made small streams that disappeared down drainage holes. Scattered about were smaller isolated boxes. It seemed as though the actual power to make the big machines work originated from these smaller boxes. She watched as Pitts, in energy form, flashed from machine to machine in a heartbeat, obviously checking them out as he went. She was sure no one else would notice him, but she was, by this time, used to the almost-transparent fields that the lightning men gave off. What's more, she could not hear any voices near them at this time. The room appeared to be presently empty of workers. She had heard voices before. Had they moved to a different room?

Another moment, and Pitts was beside her once again. He grabbed her arm and solidified, pointing to another machine closest to them, one that looked bigger and more essential to the complex of machines around them. She motioned her open hand forward. The two rushed over to it.

Captain Melog was standing in an at-ease position, his shoulders turned to the walls, his back facing the open hallway leading down to the main dining and entrance room. He was not thinking or moving, just standing, ready to strike if needed. Lady Silyaac had said to give the prisoners time to talk and make arrangements. There was no way out of the room except by the locked door that Melog could clearly see at the end of the hallway. He was a good soldier who needed no food or sleep and who followed his orders completely. If he could feel pride, that's what he would be feeling right now. But, as far as he could tell, he couldn't feel any of those kinds of emotions. He had tried from time to time. There were moments when he thought that something, indeed, was stirring up deep inside of him, some new kind of experience he had never noticed before. But it had turned out to be simply a reaction to some physical stimulus or a particular kind of thinking process taking place. Still, he thought that some of those feelings could eventually happen. He might, in fact, become more alive, more human, as time went on. And time, apparently, was something that he had a lot of.

Turning, he could hear men's voices coming down the hallway behind him. But that was impossible. The machinery workers were all on the lower level. They were not allowed up here on Lady Silyaac's level, under strict orders. He looked back in the direction of Kaal Bood's and Cathyn's room. The door was locked. They had no weapons. They'd be secure while he checked this out. Turning again, he walked down the hallway.

Cathyn and Pitts stood in front of the control panel facing one of the largest of the generators. There was a pad with different kinds of numbers and symbols on it in the middle of the panel, with gauges on either side, presumably to measure power and pressure coming from the machine. The needles were vibrating in the middle of the dials.

"I don't understand these things at all," Cathyn whispered.

Pitts grabbed on to Cathyn's arm and again sparked into solid form. Smoothing down the edges of his goatee, he sniffed twice, looked at the panel, at the generator, and then back at the panel again.

"Tell me you understand how this works," Cathyn whispered, looking at the prospector.

"Well, now, mum...can't say as I knows how these newfangled machines work, but if it's anything like the old ones I'm used to working on"—he smiled a knowing smile at Cathyn—"I thinks I can figure it out. That steam there tells me the whole thing's probably steam-driven. Not a fancy setup."

He craned his neck to look around at the back of the panel. Then he got down on his knees. Cathyn, still being held on to, was forced down to the floor with him. Together they crawled along on the floor between the control panel and the generator. There was a slight gap between the floor and the machine. Pitts seemed to be following one or two of the fat cables that snaked out from the panel and led into the large metal contraption. Once they got to the base of it, the lightning man let go of Cathyn's arm and disappeared into the machine itself with a pop, leaving Cathyn sitting on the floor. What could he be doing in there? He couldn't touch or move anything inside.

Just then, Cathyn heard a squeak on the floor just to her right and behind her. She turned her head and saw a man in a white uniform with a black-edged mask standing next to the control panel. He was looking at her.

Melog turned the corner of the hallway and saw a body lying facedown. It was one of the machine workers. He walked up to him, bent down, and felt the man's pulse near the neck. He was still alive, but unconscious. Melog looked around the hallway. No other clues. What was this man doing on the upper floor? And why was he unconscious? Had there been a gas leak of some kind? Maybe he had run up here to get to safety or to warn Silyaac. Melog sniffed the air.

While a dangerous gas could not affect him, his senses were highly tuned. If there was poison gas in the air, he could detect it. Nothing. He turned back to the unconscious machine worker. He remembered that he had heard more than one voice earlier. This was not good.

Kettle and Gamliggy were, meanwhile, vibrating furiously through wall after wall of the first floor of the fortress. They were like energy bands let loose in an asteroid belt, hit face-first by the walls as they zapped their way through them. They were traveling at near light speed, a thing that they had discovered they could do in the forest. At this speed, the world seemed to be standing still. As they entered each room, they swung their gazes throughout, looking for Cathyn's and Kaal Bood's weapons.

"I loves that trick with the machine worker, Kettle!" panted Gamliggy as they continued to race through the rooms.

"Yeah, a nice bit of work, that one," agreed Kettle. "Too bad for him he had to find us on that lower level. One vibratin' pinch on the temple, and it's like he's been kicked in the head by a workhorse."

"And then to move him up to this level for old Captain to find him?" Gamliggy grinned. "Pure genius. Captain will be tryin' to put that one together for a nigh high time!"

"Yeah, well, it should give us a few more minutes at least to do our bit of running a...Hold on a bit—" Kettle stopped abruptly, and Gamliggy pulled up alongside him.

They were inside a large room that gleamed with shields and swords and armor that hung on the walls and lay on tables.

"Well, Gamliggy. What does you think the odds are that the misses' weapons would be in the weapons room?"

"I don't know. Three to one?"

Kettle sighed. "I didn't mean that as a real question."

"Well, what'd you ask me for?"

"It's a rhetorical question."

"A reorbital question?" asked Gamliggy. "Is that a question that comes around again for another try?"

"A rhetorical question," corrected Kettle. "It's a question that you asks when you don't expects an answer."

Gamliggy scratched his head. His eyes squinted up. "Well, why in the world would you asks a question that you wouldn't want your mate to answer?"

Kettle patted Gamliggy on the shoulder. He smiled and nodded his head. "You're a good mate, Gamliggy. Now, remind me where we put that second bloke we cuffed a bit ago."

"Who are you?" the machine worker asked, looking down at Cathyn sitting on the floor.

Cathyn stood up slowly. "I'm new here," she said calmly. "Captain Melog sent me down to get a uniform."

The man looked at Cathyn suspiciously. "Lady Silyaac's never hired a woman before. And you're just a girl."

The words made the hairs on the back of her neck stand up. Cathyn bowed her head a bit so that the worker wouldn't see how nervous she was. She looked back up with a confident stare. "I'm an engineer. My name's Cathyn. I'm a bit of a genius, you see. Graduated early. Lady Silyaac hired me to... inspect the...generators. She told me that there had been some problems recently...something about the temperature in the fortress being too uncomfortable for her. Now, if you want, I can go back up and tell her that I'm running into some problems down here. What was your name?"

The worker was still sizing her up. He was mulling over this last bit of information. If it were true, he'd be in trouble with Silyaac, which would not be a good thing. If the girl was lying and she was an intruder, it'd be a feather in his cap to have captured her.

Cathyn maintained eye contact with the man. But, behind him and to his right, Cathyn saw, out of the corner of her eye, a hazy disturbance in the air. It was moving slowly around his back and now toward his left side. Just as the man was about to speak, a part of the disturbance, in a rush, moved toward the man's temple at the side of his head. There was a loud pop, and the worker crumpled to the ground. Cathyn walked quickly toward him as the shimmering figure grabbed his arm.

"Is he dead?" Cathyn asked.

"No, just knocked out a bit," Pitts replied, now solid again. He looked at Cathyn. "A nice technique we learned a while back. Poke our finger right here at the temple"—Pitts pointed—"and they're out for hours. Kettle says it's like a shock of some kind. Bit handy to have around, wouldn't you say?"

"I would say. I don't think he was believing me." She tilted her head toward the prone worker.

"Beggin' your pardon, miss, but I wasn't believin' you neither. Sad story, that," said Pitts, smiling.

"I thought it was all right under the circumstances." Cathyn smiled back. "What about the generator?"

"I thinks I got that one covered. Checked it out from the inside."

"How can you stop it? You can't actually touch anything while you're in that super-fast state. And another thing...how come you don't just fall through the floor when you're like that?"

"Now that's a good question, mum," said Pitts, looking serious. "Kettle showed us a while back that we can walks through solid objects all right, but we gotta thinks about it. It don't come natural-like, you see. Whereas just standin' here, we don't disturb nothin' in the solid world." He gave her a funny half smile. "Does that make sense?"

"It does...sort of."

Pitts looked serious again. "Well, my idea for this here generator is just a theory, but I thinks it's a good one." He gave Cathyn a wink. "Let's see if it works. Best stand back, though. Be ready for a little explosion. Don't know when this thing'll blow." He released his hand from the worker and vibrated into the air. Cathyn watched as he walked through the generator for a second time.

Backing up and pulling the worker along the floor by his arms, Cathyn stood between the unconscious man and the generator that Pitts was now tinkering with. She could hear intense crackling from inside the box. Then there was quiet. For just a few seconds.

The explosion was a shock. Much more powerful than Cathyn expected. It blew her back onto the worker whom Pitts had knocked out. His unconscious body gave her a soft landing, not waking him up in the slightest. When she looked back up, Cathyn could see through a haze of black smoke that the whole front side of the generator had been blown off.

CHAPTER 16
EXPLOSION

Melog felt the explosion through the floor. He stood up from the unconscious man and ran, instinctively, down the corridor, toward the room where Cathyn and Kaal Bood were being held. Checking the door, he noticed that it was still locked. Time to look inside later. Right now he had to get down to the lower level. That's where it felt like the explosion had come from. Turning away from the door and pulling his sword, he ran, full tilt, down the hallway, toward the stairs.

"Blimey! What was that?!" Gamliggy exclaimed when they heard the explosion.

"Pitts and Cathyn," Kettle answered. "Guess they've started their business. Best we get a move on."

They heard another explosion, and then another, and then a fourth in quick succession.

"Quite a job they's doin' down there." Gamliggy smiled.

The two lightning men were dragging another unconscious machine worker along the floor by his arms. The man was on his back. On his stomach lay Cathyn's bow, her quiver of arrows, her longsword in its scabbard, her knife and shin strap, a shield, a battle-ax, a mace, two other longswords, and three wide daggers. The weight of the load was clearly making progress difficult.

"Good Lord, Gamliggy," puffed Kettle. "Did you have to grab the entire armory?"

"Well, it seemed a shame to leave all that rot in there," Gamliggy wheezed. "Some of these things may come in handy. You never know."

"Yeah, well, in the meantime, it's making us slow as tortoises."

The prospectors turned a corner and glanced down the hallway.

"Hey, Kettle…Captain's gone," whispered Gamliggy.

"Musta run down to check out the explosions. Hurry up. Let's get these weapons down to Cathyn's room."

They pulled up on the man's arms again and continued down the hallway, zigzagging the unconscious worker along like a fat snake as they went.

"Kettle, tell me one more time…Why'd we need this bloke?"

Kettle continued pulling and sighed. If his hand had been freed, he'd have rubbed it hard across his face in exasperation. "One more time, Gamliggy," he grunted. "We needed this here bloke so's that we could get the weapons back to Cathyn and her mum."

Gamliggy gave that some thought. "Yes, well…why put all the stuff on his tummy and slide him around like a mop?"

Kettle gave a sound very close to a growl. "Because we can't touch the weapons, can we?" he said between gritted teeth.

"I touched the weapons," Gamliggy said.

"I know you touched the weapons, but you couldn't have touched the weapons without touchin' this here sleepin' bloke."

Gamliggy squinted a bit. "But what's with the all the slidin'?"

Kettle sniffed. "We had to put the weapons on him so that we could move them. As long as we're touchin' him, we can move him. If we can move him, we can move the weapons. So we puts the weapons on him, and now we're usin' him like a wagon. That's why, when I held on to his hand, and you held on to my hand, you was able to grab the weapons and give them to me so I could put them on his tummy. We had to make a livin' connection in order to become solid. Now do you get it?" Kettle looked over at Gamliggy, who was scrunching up his brows in deep thought.

"Look," he continued, "even though the bloke was unconscious, he was still a livin' bloke, so we was able to do our solid thing, and him not even knowin' he was helpin' out."

Gamliggy was nodding his head. He stopped nodding and looked at Kettle. "But why all the sliding?"

They had reached a room that was just down the hall from Cathyn and Kaal Bood's cell. Kettle stopped, forcing Gamliggy to pull up. He took a deep breath and continued on. "Does you like the slidin', Gamliggy?"

"I like the slidin', Kettle. It's like pushin' around a mop, 'cept this one's got arms."

"Gamliggy, just be glad that we're back with the weapons and you don't have to thinks about it no more."

"Oh, I'm glad of that, all right." Gamliggy flashed a broad grin. "Kettle?"

"What?"

"Can I push him a bit more down the hallway?"

"No, you cannot," Kettle growled. He continued holding on to the worker's arm as he opened the door.

Cathyn looked over her shoulder and saw an area on the floor that was shimmering slightly. She crawled over to it. She could hear the distinctive hum of Pitts in super-fast form.

"Pitts. Pitts," she said.

A dark black smoke was billowing out from the four machines that Pitts had apparently sabotaged. An alarm of some kind had been set off somewhere. Cathyn could hear furious running and voices shouting. The second generator that Pitts had sabotaged had been located in the next room over. The work crew was obviously busy with that one. Hopefully, they would think that was the only one until they began a fuller inspection.

Cathyn reached over and touched the energy form. It solidified into Pitts, half sitting up and shaking his head.

"Pitts…how did you do that? How did you blow those generators?"

The prospector's eyes rolled back down from inside his head. "Whew! That last one nearly got me."

"What happened?" Cathyn pressed on. They were both now sitting on the floor, side by side.

"Well…I noticed once I got inside them machines that there's only one movin' part, really. It's this contraption of coils that spins around. The section where it spins around was hummin' like what we does, like it's made up of the same lightnin' stuff like us. I figure it's these spinnin' coils that make the power."

"What did you do?"

"It was easy, really. All I done was stick me hand inside that hummin', cracklin' area where them coils was spinnin', and…kaboom! My energy body musta interfered with what them coils was doin'. I done the same thing to that one in the other room, and then these other two next to this one." Pitts started to rub the back of his head. "I got outs plenty early for them first three, but this last one nearly got me."

"But you aren't hurt at all," Cathyn breathed. "Not a scratch."

"Well, I was in me energy form, wasn't I? The explosions blew me over here, but it was just like I was a blob of warm air hitchin' a ride on a cold breeze. I was out of the first one before it blew, and already workin' on the other three."

Cathyn looked at the lightning man fondly. "Well," she began, "that was brilliant. Well done."

Pitts stopped rubbing his head and smiled.

They could hear the sound of frantic running footsteps and yelling voices coming closer. "Time to go," Cathyn said, standing up. She released her hold on the prospector, leaving him energized once again.

Silyaac had also heard the explosions. Sitting in her reading chair, going over her plans in her daybook, she had stood up suddenly, dropping the book to the floor. It lay facedown, opened at the page she was reading. She had discovered not too long ago that she could still read and write by using her fingers to move across the pages, feeling the slight indentations that the ink had left on the paper. The magic that was inside her shape-changing body had, apparently, given her fingers extraordinary sensitivity after she was blinded by the fireball at the Battle of the Suns.

Still standing, she closed her eyes and brought up a hazy image of Captain Melog. She was still able to do this, but the effect was slowly fading, no doubt brought on by her blindness. She could see in her mind's eye Melog's blurred figure moving quickly. There were other figures around him. He was on the bottom floor amongst the machinery. A sense of confusion and anger emanated from the image.

"Melog," she whispered.

The figure in her mind's eye stopped, dropped his head as if listening. "Yes, my lady," he said.

She could not hear any other sounds that were around him. His voice that she now heard was simply the voice in his own head.

"What's happening?" she asked.

"Apparently four of the generators blew down here. We're checking into it now. One of the workers is unconscious nearby. Perhaps he was trying to bring down the pressure when they blew. Strange, though..."

"What's strange?"

"He's not injured, no sign of him being in the explosion at all. But he's far enough away, it looks like it blew him backward."

Silyaac thought about this. "Kaal Bood and her daughter..." she said.

"I checked the door before coming down here. It's still locked. They couldn't have gotten out."

Silyaac wet her lips with her tongue. "Let the workers continue checking out the machines. You get back to that cell. Open the door. Tell me what you find."

"Yes, my lady."

The image dissolved.

By the time Kettle and Gamliggy had materialized inside the cold sleep cell, a haze of smoke was already working its way in through the hole, threatening to fill up the room. It was turning blacker and thicker with each heartbeat.

Kettle found Kaal Bood near the door, pacing. He touched her arm. "Cathyn and Pitts back yet?" he asked.

Even as he said this, they heard someone grunting near the hole in the floor.

Cathyn was pulling herself up through the hole, smoke wafting over her body, following her in. She kneeled, facing away from the smoke, breathing hard. "I can't get Pitts up," she panted.

The other three looked down into the hole. Peering through the smoke, they saw the energy form of Pitts standing on top of one of the machines. Kettle and Gamliggy could tell that he was looking up at them.

"I was able to stand on his shoulders." Cathyn gulped. "He pushed me up to the hole, but now he can't get up himself."

A static-like sound issued from Pitts. Kettle, still touching Kaal Bood's arm, nodded. "He says he's gonna go back down into the generator room and around and up through the walls. He says not to worry, no one will be able to spot him, that he'll be back up in a tick."

"The weapons," Kaal Bood whispered.

"They're hidden just outside the door," Kettle answered. "Just as you get out in the hallway."

"How will we get to them?" Cathyn asked.

"Well…I figure Melog's got to check in on you two pretty soon here," Kettle continued, "and when he does, that's when we makes our move."

"It can't be too soon." Cathyn coughed, motioning at the smoke that was now filling up the room. "If he doesn't open up that door soon, we'll suffocate."

They heard a loud click and turned their heads. The door was opening.

CHAPTER 17
MELOG

Once the door was opened, the smoke immediately flushed toward it, like a snake slithering down a hole. Cathyn, Kaal Bood, and the two lightning men could see a figure standing in the middle of the doorway, obscured by the black smoke that was wafting over it.

Kettle and Gamliggy didn't waste any time. Releasing his grip on Kaal Bood, Kettle ran toward the open door, followed by Gamliggy. The figure stepped into the room.

Now they could see that it was, indeed, Captain Melog, sword in hand, ready for an attack.

Kettle reached him first, blasting him in the side of his head with his energy touch. It knocked him sideways onto the floor, away from the door.

Gamliggy fell on top of him, instantly assuming solid shape. "Last doorway on the right!" he yelled at Cathyn and Kaal Bood as they bolted from the room. "Don't worry about us! We'll be—"

But he was swept off the prone guard with a mighty heave. Gamliggy energized in midair and then was solid again as Captain Melog held him down on his back with his black-gloved hand wrapped firmly around his throat.

"Get out of this, lightning man," he hissed as he tightened his grip.

Gamliggy was coughing violently, losing his breath. Melog moved his head from side to side, at the ready for the remaining lightning man to attack, sword arm cocked. Too late. Kettle, still in energy form, zapped him with another explosive shot in the temple, knocking him off the prospector.

Gamliggy could barely breathe. "Just in the nick," he gasped to Kettle, both now in energy form.

The gray guard stood up, ready again for battle. He approached the two energy beings. A look of pure hate and determination played across his face.

In a shot, the two prospectors split up in different directions, crackling through the left and right walls of the cell.

Captain Melog looked back and forth from one wall to the other, listening intently. Moments passed. Silence. Had they run? No more time to waste. The escaped prisoners need to be tended to.

Suddenly from above, Kettle, still in lightning form, dropped through the ceiling and landed on Melog's back. He solidified at the moment of contact.

The combination of the intense shock of energy and the now-solid and full weight of the burly prospector knocked the gray guard to the floor, on his face. He landed with an "Oomph!"

Kettle remained sitting on him. The prospector kicked the sword out of Melog's hand. Captain Melog roared and pushed himself off of the floor with a mighty heave. Kettle rolled off his back and crackled into energy again, continuing to roll right through the floor and out of sight. The guard stood up.

Another intense shock to his left backed the unarmed guard up against the wall. It was Gamliggy this time, appearing suddenly from the wall that he had dissipated into. Melog was quick to pick up his sword and go after the thin lightning man. The gray guard began hacking away at his opponent. It was like a well-rehearsed dance. Captain Melog would slice at Gamliggy. The sword would crackle through nothing, doing no harm. Then Gamliggy would thump the gray man in the chest with an intense energy punch, knocking the breath out of him. Slice. Crackle. Punch. Slice. Crackle. Punch. Melog's sword was knocked out of his hand on this last punch. Just as quickly, the guard grabbed Gamliggy's arm, solidified him, and rendered his own punch to the prospector's head. Gamliggy went down in an energy clump on the floor.

As Melog approached Gamliggy for a final blow, two hands unexpectedly shot up out of the floor beneath and behind him and grabbed hold of his ankles. The right hand lifted the right foot forward and sent the guard tumbling to the floor. The hands disappeared as Gamliggy got up and reoriented himself. Kettle suddenly appeared by his friend's side. They were just about to apparate out of the cell when the inanimate suddenly grabbed them both from behind, by their necks, forcing them back to their solid bodies. He banged their heads against the nearest wall and let them crumple to the floor.

The mother-and-daughter warriors had run out of the door and turned right. Reaching the last cell door, they opened it to reveal their weapons piled on the floor, one on top of another, an unconscious worker laying nearby. Kaal Bood went to grab her old bow and quiver and met Cathyn's hand under her own. They looked at one another. Kaal Bood pulled her hand back and grabbed a longsword and a wide dagger instead. For an instant, Cathyn did not move. Then she slung the bow and quiver around her shoulder. She picked up her own longsword and holstered it about her waist. She also grabbed one of the wide daggers as well. She tucked this into her belt. The silent exchange had left her breathing hard. When she turned to run back to help Kettle and Gamliggy, Melog was out of the cell, standing in the hallway.

"A wall to your backs, and me in front," he said. "Your only escape is through me now, and I'm not going to let that happen."

"You're facing two seasoned warriors, Melog!" Kaal Bood announced. "We can take you!"

Captain Melog spat on the ground. "Then take me," he hissed.

Faster than reflex, Cathyn had an arrow nocked and flying toward Melog's chest. Just as fast, Melog deflected it with his sword. His head was turned slightly, as if he were listening to every move they made. Again, Cathyn let an arrow fly, and again it was deflected by Melog, who was still turned and listening hard, almost not looking. His reflexes were astounding, Cathyn thought. He was slowly backing up so that Cathyn and Kaal Bood's cell was now in front of him. He was expecting Kettle and Gamliggy to recover and come out of the room soon. He wanted them in front of him.

Kaal Bood let a wide dagger fly at the gray man. He caught it in midair, flipping it, now worthless, to the ground.

"We can do this all day!" he yelled. "Show me the warrior you are, Commander! Come at me!"

Suddenly, an energy field crackled through the wall to Melog's left and blasted him to the floor. A pulsating figure was glistening in the hallway, looking down at Melog. It was Pitts, up from the machine room. The static that was the lightning men's high-speed speech announced something indecipherable to all who could hear it. Two other energy fields glided out from the room and merged with the lone one in the hallway. The static-talk continued.

Melog was trying to stand up, but the effort seemed to be too much for him. Cathyn was ready with another arrow if he decided to try a sudden move. Maybe if she could catch him while he was distracted, he wouldn't be able to deflect those arrows. But she would wait till he was up. Shooting a struggling warrior on the ground was not in her nature. He was eyeing the lightning men intensely. He did not want another one of those head explosions.

"Keep Captain Melog here!" Kaal Bood yelled toward the lightning men. "Cathyn and I will head toward the main entrance. As soon as you can, follow us!"

They turned and began their jog down the corridor, when they saw another figure walking toward them. It was Captain Melog.

CHAPTER 18
DUEL

This Captain Melog was walking slowly, carefully, sizing up the situation as he approached, but not backing down—just the way a good soldier would do it. He drew his longsword and stopped to eye the other Captain Melog who was half sitting, half lying on the floor.

Without taking the time to work out this second Captain Melog, Cathyn let fly with another arrow. This time it hit him right in the chest, dead center. He staggered back half a step. He had not been fast enough this time to deflect it. A fragment of a heartbeat later, another arrow followed, hitting the inanimate in the shoulder. Another in the stomach. Yet another in the chest again. With each shot, he staggered backward on his feet a bit, until the volley of arrows stopped. Maintaining eye contact with Cathyn and Kaal Bood, he methodically pulled out each arrow, starting with the highest one in his shoulder and working his way down his body. He threw the arrows on the floor. They hit with a clatter and rolled.

Cathyn and Kaal Bood looked back at the shimmer of the lightning men and the other Melog on the floor. They watched as the figure seemed to drain himself of color, like someone spraying a fresh painting with water, the paint dripping off in pools and disappearing on the floor. The details washed off of the body, leaving it in the shape of Silyaac. She slowly got up and stumbled past Cathyn and her mother, toward the real Melog. They watched, astonished.

"Do not try and touch her," Melog warned. He held out his arm and pulled Silyaac into him, holding on to her. She put her own arm, closest to him, around his shoulders.

"I cannot let you leave," she panted, now in the safety of her trusted guard. "I cannot remain in this darkness any longer. I will not remain in this darkness any longer. One of you will give up your eyes for me, or I will kill you both."

Cathyn and her mother turned to a sound behind them. The energy field that was the three lightning men suddenly separated. One-third of it disappeared through the right wall, from where they were standing; the other two-thirds went through the left wall. Silence filled the hallway. Melog looked from one wall to the other, then back at Cathyn and Kaal Bood.

"They're coming back through the walls," Silyaac panted. "Their energy blasts…"

Melog understood. Pulling Silyaac in tighter to his body, he turned and took off down the hallway, toward the main entrance. Even carrying a body, he was running at incredible speed.

Cathyn and Kaal Bood followed after him, weapons in hand. Melog ran full-out. He was heading somewhere specific.

Cathyn watched as she ran. He was carrying Silyaac as if she were a sack of cloth over his shoulder. They turned up another corridor, running past the main entrance. Where were they going?

"Mother!" yelled Cathyn. Kaal Bood stopped running. Cathyn also stopped and turned toward her mother. "Head toward the main entrance! Try and find a way out! I'll get back to you!"

Kaal Bood looked questioningly at her daughter.

"Silyaac's got to be destroyed now while she's vulnerable!" Cathyn continued. "This is an opportunity that we cannot let pass! You must find an escape route; then come back around from another side. You'll be my reinforcements."

Like a good soldier, Kaal Bood turned into the room.

Cathyn continued her run. She was in good shape. Even with all of the weapons on her body, she was barely winded. She felt like she could have run the perimeter of the castle and back again.

When she turned another bend, Melog and Silyaac were gone. No sign of them down the hallway.

Cathyn slowed to a stop. She looked around her. There was no movement, no sounds. Only her own breathing. She continued walking in the same direction that she had been running.

The hallway seemed to be winding upward. It was spiraling in a subtle curve that she knew was leading her to the roof of the fortress. Perhaps that was not a bad place to go, to be able to see what was around them and then find another way out. Whether or not it was where Melog and Silyaac had run, she could not be sure.

Her longsword in her hand, she picked up her running again until she finally came to one last door. It was open slightly. She could smell the ocean air just on the other side. She pushed the door so that it swung all the way open and waited.

It was almost night. Cathyn could see just a slice of the sky from where she stood. A full moon lit up an otherwise dark scene on the other side of the door. The moon was very bright. No clouds. She couldn't hear any rain. It had stopped. Still, no movement from either side. She could hear ocean birds squawking around the top of the fortress. Were they making noise because someone was there or because they had the roof all to themselves? Strange that this would lead to the roof of the fortress; it didn't seem as though she had climbed high enough. More magic?

With her back to the door, Cathyn glided through sideways, turning slowly toward her right. She knew how to make herself a smaller target.

Suddenly, she swung her sword arm in a lightning-quick arc, making contact with a large shadow that had been pressed against the wall, next to the open door. Melog's head thumped to the ground and rolled just past her feet. After a moment's hesitation, his body collapsed against the wall. There was a sword line cut into the wall against which Melog had stood, but no blood decorated it.

Cathyn heard a groan from behind her. Turning, she saw Silyaac crumpled on the floor of the roof, her head in her hands.

"You've ruined everything," she hissed. "Three years' worth of plans, and you've ruined them."

She looked at the white sorceress seemingly defeated on her knees. "We're leaving now, Silyaac," Cathyn panted. "I'm going to turn around and go back down to find my mother and the lightning men. Then we're going out one of your doors, with or without your help. If we can't find one, we'll make one. I'm sure the lightning men can find a way out."

"You're just a girl, and you've ruined everything," she continued. "How could that happen?"

"You underestimated your enemies, Silyaac. The Academy taught me to never do that."

Silyaac pulled her face out of her hands. "And you've overestimated your strengths, Cathyn." Silyaac tilted her head in the warrior's direction and brought her hands up in the air in front of her.

Cathyn felt her legs trembling. What was this? Her feet left the floor, and she was floating. Slowly she rose into the air. Now she was dangerously high above the floor of the roof. If she were to fall at this height, she'd break an arm or a leg or her back.

Silyaac shifted her hands sideways, toward her left. Cathyn moved slightly to the right, toward the edge of the roof. Within a moment, she was dangling in midair just away from the fortress. The sky was a dark blue with darker clouds moving in close to the full moon. She could see the rocks and the water walkway below. Now she was high enough for death.

She tried to swing her sword arm at the bubble around her, but found that her other muscles were experiencing mild spasms, making her unable to move them. It was like she was wrapped up in the same power that ran the generators below.

"How are you doing this?" Cathyn screamed from high in the air. "You're a shape-shifter! You said you have no control over material objects like your sister had!"

"It's true!" Silyaac yelled back. "Ordinarily I can't control objects around me! But in this instance…it's different!" She was panting now.

Cathyn could feel her body shaking as it dipped and swayed in the air. Was Silyaac losing control? Was the weight too much for her to hold up Cathyn for too long? "Why is this any different?"

Silyaac allowed herself a smile. "This is my high card, as it were! Do you remember your fight with the gulunay?"

"How did you know about that?"

"I arranged it!" Silyaac continued. "And the singing stones? And the waterlings?"

"You arranged for me to…what? Fight them? But I didn't fight the singing stones!"

"No, but you touched them, didn't you? Like you touched the gulunay and the waterlings, and even the lightning men!"

"The lightning men were a part of this?"

Silyaac laughed. "Yes, they were, poor things! Unbeknownst to them! Although I didn't expect them to follow you here! That was another miscalculation!"

Cathyn adjusted her position in the air. "What about the Murdered Man?"

The white witch thought about this. "Not my doing," she said at last. "Sounds interesting, though. Something extra, I imagine. Icing on the cake. Just for you, my young warrior."

Cathyn's body shifted again in the air. The movements reminded her how tenuous her position was, that she could drop at any moment. "How could just touching all those things cause this to happen?"

"Did you learn about the four basic elements at the Academy?" asked Silyaac, now obviously straining under the weight of controlling Cathyn's body.

Cathyn was finding it difficult to keep up a running conversation while hovering erratically in midair. "Air...fire...earth...water!" As she said it, she knew how Silyaac had done it.

"There you have it—the gulunay took care of the air, the lightning men were the fire, the singing stones were the earth, and the waterlings were the water! I devised a spell that allows me to telekinetically control your body once you came into contact with all those things! That's why I had Melog bring you here along the path he took! That's why he conveniently disappeared or, in the case of the lightning men, allowed himself to go along with the setup! I love the simplicity of it all! Here's a lesson for you, Cathyn—if you ever survive this particular dilemma—always have a backup plan, preferably a good one!"

"So...what are you going to do now, kill me or lecture me?" Cathyn shouted.

"That all depends on your mother! Ahhh...speak of the devil, here she comes now!"

CHAPTER 19
HIGH CARD

Behind Cathyn and to her left, she saw Kaal Bood run through the doorway, sword in hand. A large energy field was close behind her. The lightning men.

It took the mother warrior seconds to assess the situation—Melog's head on the floor, Silyaac kneeling, her hands in the air, Cathyn suspended in the air past the roofline, above the rocks.

"Release her now, Silyaac!" Kaal Bood shouted. She walked toward the white sorceress, her sword pointed at her enemy.

Silyaac laughed. "Or what, Kaal, you'll cut off my head like my poor captain? I don't think so. Consider the consequences. I have your daughter dangling hundreds of meters over rocks that will surely kill her the moment I release her." Her voice changed, now steady and demanding. "Put your sword down!"

There was no movement.

"Now!" she spat, turning her head in Kaal Bood's direction.

The warrior woman threw the sword in front of her. It landed, flat side down, bouncing slightly as it hit.

"And tell your energy friends there to stay put. I heard them as they came through the doorway, and I will hear them if they attempt to separate. The moment they do that, your daughter drops."

The energy field that was the lightning men hummed, but remained still. All eyes were on Silyaac and Cathyn.

"I'm all right, Mother!" Cathyn yelled. "I'm prepared to die! Don't give in to her!" And then, "Pick up your sword! The moment that she releases me from this force field, use it to cut off her head!"

Kaal Bood knew that she could not do that. "So, this is where the deal makes its final stand, eh, Silyaac?"

"Precisely, Kaal. Here it is, a deal that you cannot refuse. Give me your eyes willingly, or your daughter dies."

"But I'll kill you the moment you let her go."

Silyaac was moving her head back and forth, thinking. "Kaal, you're dealing with someone who has nothing to lose. Remember what your teachers taught you? I'm the most dangerous kind of enemy right now. And I'm gambling that you'll choose your daughter's life for your eyes."

Kaal Bood breathed deeply.

"She stays enclosed in this force field until you and I complete the deal," Silyaac continued. "Am I wrong?"

Another breath from the warrior woman. "You're not wrong, Silyaac. I'll give you my eyes willingly."

"Check and mate," whispered Silyaac.

"No! Mother! I won't let you!" Cathyn cried. She wriggled, trying to get herself free from the grasp of the energy that was flowing from Silyaac's hands. If she could, she would have flung herself from the top of the fortress. Silyaac's hold on her remained strong.

The lightning men shifted and hummed. The light that surrounded them fluctuated, along with their feelings of helplessness.

Kaal Bood looked intently at Silyaac. "You'll have to bring her down to the floor to begin the transfer."

Silyaac studied that idea. "I'll put her down, but she'll remain in the bubble during the process."

Cathyn heard all of this as if she were in a dream, these two people talking about her in third person. It was as if she weren't there, as if she didn't matter. And her utter helplessness, it infuriated her. She could feel the back of her neck grow hot. She suddenly dropped her sword. It fell through the energy field and landed with a clang on the stone of the rooftop floor. The hairs on her arms stood up. She curled her fingers into two fists, her short fingernails digging into the flesh of her palms. She gritted her teeth and screamed a silent but powerful scream deep inside her throat.

And then, suddenly, her limbs stiffened out. The force was so swift and so powerful that it took her breath away. All fingers, all toes were splayed out as if something was filling her up to the brim, like a balloon being blown up. A kind of force inside her chest was erupting, sending out waves of power. Cathyn took in the air in quick, evenly paced gulps. A scared and unsure sound, like a child on the verge of crying, escaped from her throat with each breath.

She could see Silyaac and her mother still talking below her, but she could not hear them. There was a buzzing going on inside of her head, and she could hear her own breathing, her own heart pumping blood furiously through her veins, her own tiny cries of surprise as each new feeling took hold.

Cathyn closed her eyes and drew her body tight into a ball, knees up, arms in, head down. She felt as if she could will herself down to the floor of the rooftop. And slowly, very slowly, she felt herself floating down. She looked like a baby in the womb, falling from the sky in a flashing yellow ball. This was not Silyaac's doing. This was her, Cathyn! She was now in control of the very force in which Silyaac had her.

She knew that the talking had stopped, even though she could not hear any of it. She knew that all eyes and ears were turned toward her as she lightly touched the floor, Silyaac's energy field still surrounding her. She unwrapped herself and stood to her full height, eyes still closed. She was listening to the new sounds in her body. They were talking to her. A new body, and it was talking to her, telling her what to do next.

She opened her eyes and, in one sudden movement, swung her arms outward to her sides. Instantly, and with a loud crack, Silyaac's energy field disappeared.

There was silence. Even Cathyn had stopped breathing. It had been so simple. Cathyn felt that she had known how to do it all along, but that she'd been in a sleep. But now she was awake. And now she knew what she could do.

Silyaac could tell what had happened. She could hear Cathyn's feet as they touched the floor, hear Cathyn's arms as they moved suddenly out from the center of her body, feel the energy field fall away. "She's a sorceress!" she yelled.

The lapping of the waves around the bottom of the fortress added to the tension in the air. Kaal Bood picked up her sword and walked toward Silyaac. She turned the sword so that the point was at Silyaac's throat.

"There's no way she could have broken that spell," Silyaac hissed. "It was negotiated with the four elements. It was an elemental. There's no spell stronger than the elementals!" She turned her face in the direction of the adult warrior. "Kaal," she continued, laughing now, "you have a sorceress for a daughter."

Kaal Bood seemed to have no reaction to this. "I should kill you where you kneel," she whispered through gritted teeth. "Get up, Silyaac. Show us how to get out of here. We're going home."

"A sorceress for a daughter!" Silyaac laughed again. It echoed around the diameter of the rooftop, the only sound besides the waves and the wind. It was a self-satisfied laugh, as if Silyaac had won the battle, not the group who now had her under their weapons.

Mother and daughter looked at one another. Cathyn knew it to be true, and now, judging by the look on her mother's face, knew that her mother knew as well.

"How long have you known?" Cathyn hissed.

"This is not the time to discuss this," Kaal Bood whispered.

"This is the perfect time to discuss this," Cathyn continued. "Not another moment of secrecy."

Kaal Bood sighed deeply, her sword still steadied on Silyaac's throat. "Silyaac will use this diversion to try to escape. I cannot tell you this history and guard her as well." She nodded at the figure sitting defeated at her feet.

Cathyn turned to the blind sorceress and raised one hand. She turned her palm so that it pointed directly at Silyaac. Closing her eyes, Cathyn envisioned an energy field running from her hand to Silyaac's body. She felt a tingle. When she opened her eyes, Silyaac was kneeling in a transparent bubble. The blind sorceress was feeling the inside of the bubble with her hands, determining the size and strength of the cage that now housed her. Cathyn knew that it would hold.

"Now, tell me. How did this happen?"

Kaal Bood put down her sword and turned away from Cathyn. She walked over to the edge of the roof, put out a hand to steady herself against the battlements. Cathyn followed behind her. The wind blew their hair out at angles from their heads. Seabirds began bustling over the roof again now that the activity had stilled.

"When we discovered the portal to this world," Kaal Bood began, "we went back and forth freely, some of us on spying missions." She sighed again as she glanced far out to the ocean. "On one of these excursions over to this side, I met a man named Sheenoshta."

Cathyn's eyes filled with tears. She knew where this was going. She had been raised her whole life thinking that her father was an ordinary warrior from her own world, like her mother…and herself, that he had been killed in one of the many battles that her mother would tell her about late at night. Now an image, a story of her true father, was emerging at long last. She felt an empty space deep down in her stomach start to fill in. She hugged herself as her mother continued.

"Sheenoshta was a warrior sorcerer. He was a trusted member of the royal family who was rebelling against Lady Abathet's ruling clan." She turned back to face her daughter now. Her eyes were shining with tears that threatened to let go. "He was so handsome, so brave to be helping us overthrow that terrible and powerful family. We…fell in love." Again she was quiet, looking at Cathyn. "And then you were born."

Cathyn was perfectly silent while she took this in. Her eyes strayed from her mother to Silyaac. The white woman was still, listening to the story within Cathyn's own energy bubble.

"Someday you will tell me this entire story," Cathyn said.

Kaal Bood sighed. "Yes, someday. Soon. But not now. We must deal with this." She nodded at Silyaac, then looked back at her daughter.

Cathyn raised her arm again, opened and closed her hand, gave an angry grunt. The energy ball that surrounded Silyaac whistled and crackled. The lightning men moved back.

Cathyn closed her eyes and clenched her teeth. With another grunt and a wave of her arm, the energy ball blew apart into the air.

Kaal Bood was walking back toward the blind sorceress, her sword ready again. "You can hear me walking toward you, Silyaac. I have my sword. You will be wise not to move, not to try any sorcery. We're going to leave this place, and you're coming with us. I've decided I'm going to try you for treason against the Council."

Silyaac did not try to escape. Her body was slumped over, her hands on the stone floor. "I cannot go with you, Kaal," she whispered.

"Get up, Silyaac!" Kaal Bood barked.

The sorceress did not look up. "I cannot leave this place." She paused. "Without my eyes, I cannot leave." Then, she turned her head in Cathyn's direction. "Another mistake on your part, young apprentice. Never let your guard down." Silyaac raised her head. "You should have kept that bubble around me."

As soon as Cathyn heard that, she raised her hands for another blast of her internal energy, but it was too late. Silyaac was running toward the edge opposite of where both warriors stood. By the time Kaal Bood had taken two steps closer to her, Silyaac had turned herself backward. She dove headfirst over the edge.

Without a word between them, mother and daughter ran toward the precipice and looked over. They saw the white witch splash into the ocean water surrounding the fortress far below. They stood stock still for many moments and watched carefully for any movement breaking through the water's surface. But there was nothing, only the incessant waves lapping back and forth against the shoreline and the fortress walls.

Cathyn and her mother walked back to the roof door, followed closely by the lightning men. On the way, they passed the severed head of Captain Melog.

Cathyn looked down at it, its eyes open to the night sky. "No one is immortal," she whispered, then added, "dear heart." She walked on.

They passed through the door and into the dark, spiraling hallway.

"Mother, could Silyaac still be alive?" Cathyn asked as they walked together.

Kaal Bood grimaced. "Either way, we can't stay here. We have to leave now without her." She sighed. "I would have loved to have taken her back to our people for trial. She's long overdue for justice."

"Agreed," Cathyn sighed. "But there could still be more to this trap waiting to happen. Kettle, Gamliggy, Pitts, are you with us?"

They could hear the familiar crackle of the men nearby. Looking closely, Cathyn could make out the faint outline of three heads and shoulders against the dark walls.

"We're going out the front door, along the walkway, the way we came in," she said. "Now that Silyaac is... dead...I have a feeling that the doors will not be an issue. Be on guard, though—there are waterlings protecting the fortress. Be ready to attack anything that gets close to you from the water. They'll drag you in."

With that, Cathyn led the way out of the door and onto the walkway.

CHAPTER 20

THE FATHER

True to form, Cathyn had found Tempest just as they exited Silyaac's ocean fortress. The horse had trotted over to the group the moment he had spotted them. He nudged both Cathyn and her mother. Kaal Bood was surprised and very glad to see him. She petted his neck and spoke softly to him. Tempest remembered her touch and her voice. They found the saddle, blankets, and backpack nearby on the sand, where Cathyn had left them, and worked together to prepare Tempest for the journey home. The young warrior suggested that her mother ride the salt-and-pepper so that she could regain her strength after her long suspended sleep. Kaal Bood reluctantly agreed. The rest of the party walked along beside her.

It was very late in the evening when they finally reached the way up the mountain from the beach. Cathyn had beseeched the lightning men to go on ahead of them; she was aware of how quickly they could move in their energy forms, that there was no need to trudge along with the two human warriors.

But the prospectors had declined, Kettle stating that they'd "accompany Commander Bood and her daughter all the ways through Abathet Woods."

They had walked mostly in silence, glancing back at Silyaac's stronghold in the water as it disappeared around the bend in the sand. And now, they found themsleves sitting around a fire at night, talking, eating a wild mountain fowl and two seabirds that Cathyn had shot with her mother's bow (now Cathyn's), and drinking a warm, dark root drink that Kaal Bood had scrounged together. The ocean moved and crested to one side of them. Whenever they would stop to look, a phosphorous glint danced within the waves. Their talk was the talk of relief and safety and weariness and friendship, and there was even laughter.

Kettle, Gamliggy, and Pitts had all attached themselves to either Cathyn or Kaal Bood at one time or another. Once in a while, the men would let go to move to another position, then return to make contact and become solid again. They seemed to enjoy the sheer variety and freedom of being able to turn themselves on and off at their own whim.

"I'm telling you, Commander"—Kettle chuckled, smiling at Kaal Bood—"you should of seen the look on ol' Captain's face when your daughter went to slicin' off his head! Whoooweee! I got there just ahead of these two blokes, and I'll tell you, I never seen a person more surprised than that one. Done my soul a bit of good to see that happen. He was a bad lot, that one was."

"Right you are, Kettle," Pitts joined in. "I reckon it has something to do with the fact that the blighter thought he was immortal, that he was gonna be livin' forever. Nothing like a quick departure from this world to knock a bit of sense into you, eh?"

"Departure is right, Pitts!" laughed Gamliggy. "His head was departin' from his body!" The lightning men laughed.

Cathyn and Kaal Bood smiled at one another, as any warriors would do after a winning battle.

"Are you sure he's dead?" asked Cathyn.

"Best of my knowledge," answered Kettle, "anytime I've heard them stories of immortals, it's when their heads separate from their bodies that they enter the mortal world alongs with the rest of us."

Kaal Bood stirred the fire with a stick. "I'm not even sure that Silyaac is dead," she whispered. "My instincts tell me that she is not."

"Beggin' yer pardon, Commander," Kettle piped in, "but no one could have survived that spill from the top of that fortress into that there water."

"And if the fall didn't kill her, then them water creatures surely did," added Gamliggy.

"Hmmm, maybe," Kaal Bood whispered, sipping her drink.

Gamliggy looked thoughtful. "So that was Lady Abathet's sister what we was fightin' when we thoughts we was fightin' the Captain?"

Kettle elaborated. "Right. That's how come we solidified once he...er...she touched us. She was real. We wouldn't a got solid if the Captain touched us, him bein' unalive as he was."

"At any rate," Cathyn continued, "it's all over now." She looked at her mother, her face glowing from the dying fire. "Mother, are you sure you can find our way back home?"

"Yes," Kaal Bood sighed. She looked up in the direction of the mountain pass. "We'll need to get through and out of Abathet Woods. After that, the portal is halfway through the mountains. I know what to look for."

"And we'll help you get through them woods, mum," stated Kettle.

"Yeah," added Pitts. "We knows them woods like the backs of our hands."

"Let's sleep here then. There's no sense trying to work our way up this mountain in the dark," Cathyn offered. "And I'm so tired I could sleep sitting up."

The lightning men smiled and looked back and forth from each other and the fire. After a few minutes, Kettle cleared his throat.

"Well...here's beggin' you ladies good night. We'll detach now and...stand guard whilst you get some sleep, right, lads?"

"Right you are, Kettle!" Gamliggy answered.

And with no more fanfare than that, the prospectors released their holds and crackled into the night.

Cathyn rolled out one of her blankets. She looked at Kaal Bood and put out her open hand toward the other blanket, but her mother shook her head and stretched flat out on the ground, face turned up toward the night sky.

Cathyn settled down right next to her mother, close enough to rest her arm over her mother's waist.

For many minutes they lay there in silence, only the sound of the fire dying down and the waves lapping the shoreline nearby. Cathyn was the first to speak.

"I know what you're thinking, Mother."

"And what would that be, my darling?"

"You think I can help the men. You think I can break that spell they're under. I didn't want to tell them tonight and get their hopes up, but I think you're right. I think I can help them. It's something that I'm going to try tomorrow before we leave this beach."

"Are you sure, my darling?" Kaal Bood asked. "That's powerful magic at work there." She nodded in the direction of the prospectors.

"It's hard to explain," Cathyn whispered, "but I can feel something in my bones. I just know that I'm powerful enough to...I don't know...negate it. And I think I know how I can do it."

There was a slight pause.

"And now"—Cathyn swallowed—"tell me about my father." She shifted on her blanket, getting herself comfortable for the story that was about to come. "This would be a good time. No danger. No time constraints."

Kaal Bood was silent for many moments. She stared straight up into the night sky, at the new constellations that danced their slow and ever-changing choreography. The constellation that she looked at now was called Powack, a half man, half wolf that, legend said, had rescued a city from the monster Fistahaan. Her daughter would not know the legend, but she did.

"Yes, you deserve to hear the whole story of who you are and why you're here." She released a deep breath and clasped both hands behind her head.

"Lady Abathet's family was very strong and very old," she began, eyes still on the night sky. "You have to understand that. They had ruled here in this world for generations. As the histories tell it, the first rulers were not bad. They fought for their people and provided for them and protected them against all odds, natural and unnatural. But as they continued on in power, they became corrupt, as most rulers are wont to do. Some began to experiment with the black arts and acquaint themselves with dark wizards and evil sorcerers. They started to exploit and enslave their own people.

"And so it was, that within each age, there was born a secret force of sorcerer warriors, some related to the royal family, but supportive of the rebellion. Their job was to bring down the monarchy and replace it with a more empathetic democracy. Sheenoshta was one of those sorcerer warriors. He was also one of Lady Abathet's captains. He had been working with us in our world for many years. I had heard of him, of course, of all of his exploits, all of his spying missions, but I had never met him. Until one night when I was asked to cross over to this side and pick up a small but powerful package."

"What was the package?" Cathyn asked.

"It was a box, wrapped in black paper and sealed with wax. It was the fireball jewel that would help us later win our last victory against Lady Abathet's army, the same fireball, interestingly enough, that had destroyed Silyaac's eyes." Kaal Bood smiled. "Strange how connected things are, isn't it? And so I was entrusted to pick it up from Sheenoshta and bring it back to our army-in-waiting. It had to be in our hands once we crossed over. It had to be at the front of the attack, not behind it in Sheenoshta's hands. My mission was for it to be a simple one-on-one affair. No one else was involved.

"How were you able to cross over to this side?" Cathyn whispered. "How did you find the portal?"

"Do you know our village witch, Zia?"

Cathyn sat up on her bedroll. "I visited Zia. I asked her about what to do just before I came here."

Kaal Bood looked over at her daughter, interested. "What did she tell you?"

"Just warned me that it might be a trap. To take my weapons. To be careful."

Her mother smiled. "Leave it to Zia to let us all make our own mistakes," she whispered. "It was Zia who conjured the first portal and later showed us how to capture it and use it again as necessary. Did you know that she was once an advisor to the royal family herself?"

"Never." Cathyn was stunned.

"True. She had fallen from Lady Abathet's father's graces long ago." She looked at her daughter. "She was once his main counselor, you know."

Cathyn was speechless. She settled back down onto her blanket, lying sideways as her mother continued. She made a note to herself never again to judge people by how they looked. You never know what's lurking in their histories.

"Zia held no allegiance any longer to this side. It was she who managed to find her way to our world in the first place. Perhaps it was that first rent that started this whole mess," Kaal Bood whispered to herself.

"Anyway, I made my way through the portal, but found myself in the midst of a massive battle between Lady Abathet's army and an army of killendrills."

"Killendrills? What are they?"

"They are creatures like great apes, twice as tall as me, with explosive strength and fury. Three long tentacles run down their spines like backbones. They can use them like tails or arms to strike you down and crush you like paper. Truly terrible creatures. They attack whenever they are hungry or in need of new territory. The mountains were, apparently, getting crowded for them at that time.

"Anyway, the battle was bloody and ruthless. It looked like Lady Abathet's army was losing. As much as I hated the killendrills, I hated Lady Abathet's domination more. Perhaps this was the chance we had all needed. Perhaps this was how Lady Abathet was going to fall. So I waited in the trees and watched. I saw soldiers torn apart by the killendrills and used as battering rams against other soldiers. The sounds were the worst part of it, the anguished cries of the soldiers as they were killed in midstride, the screeching of the killendrills in their victory hails. I've seen many battles before, but none as bloody and terrifying as this one. I watched as the creatures pushed toward the army and forced them back to the castle. And just as a group of the creatures was rounding the top of the hill to take the castle, I was grabbed from behind and hoisted up onto a moving horse. Someone sat on the back of the saddle; I was on the front. The arm held its hand on my mouth as we rode through the woods, around to the other side of the hill.

"And then a male voice behind me said, 'We must stop them. You've got to help me stop them, or all our plans will be in vain.' He released his hold on my mouth.

"'How do you know I'll help you?' I said.

"'You are my contact tonight, are you not?' said the rider.

"'Sheenoshta,' I finally said. 'Let me talk to you on equal ground.'

"His horse did not slow down. It galloped up the hill, swinging a wide path behind the castle, and stopped. I swung myself down. Sheenoshta dropped to the ground. He was taller than me, with dark eyes and a black beard cut close to his face. His hair was long, much longer than my own, and he wore the mail and the armor of an officer at war. As he spoke, ghosts of cold mist lifted from his lips. I think I fell in love with him at that moment.

"'You brought your bow. Good,' he whispered. 'I need you to place yourself in any position where you can cut down the main frontal attack of that herd of killendrills.' He talked very quickly, without emotion. 'I've got thirty or so men stationed within the castle, but their eyes are not your eyes, and I need your eyes now. I've heard about your shooting. You'll need to take out as many from their flanks as you can.'

"Just a moment passed between us. I took his words not as a plea, but as an order from one soldier to another. I looked to the back of the castle, grabbed my bow, and ran to a small building that stood to the left of the main doors. It was a serviceable horse stable. No horses in it at that moment. I climbed to the top. The killendrills were just cresting the front hill. Amazingly, Sheenoshta had gotten us to the back of the castle before they had had a chance to breech the front.

"I could tell by the way they were walking that the creatures were tired from climbing the hill. I could also tell that they could not see me standing on the stable. I looked up into the night sky. A thin body of clouds was moving across a half-moon, obscuring any light that the soldiers and beasts had been using to fight by. The trees behind me covered me in shadow. And I had the high ground. This was like target practice.

"I had to be fast. I knew that once the first arrow hit its mark, their focus would turn in my direction. I picked out the first three that I could hit in quick succession. That would be three down out of what looked like forty or so more from where I was standing. Not a lot, but enough to disrupt their forward advance for a minute or two. I also thought that Sheenoshta probably had a trick up his sleeve as well. Should I wait for him to make his move or fire the first shot? I decided to wait for Sheenoshta to play his card.

"It wasn't long in coming. A blinding flash seemed to erupt from the wet grass directly in front of the killendrills. The creatures roared, backed away for a moment, and put their arms up over their eyes.

"I took advantage of their confusion and let the first arrow fly. I had nocked another one before the first one had struck its mark. It hit one of the beasts in the side of the neck. I watched the creature grab at it and fall while my second arrow buried itself into another one's head. By the time my third arrow was finding its way into a killendrill's hand, they had all turned toward the stable.

"A big one in the rear of the group roared and headed in my direction. I aimed and calmly followed his run, shooting him in the middle of the neck. The force of the shot knocked him on his back. He pulled the arrow out, but did not move once it was in his hand. I was able to fell at least five more in the moments that followed.

"Looking up, I noticed that, not only were arrows flying from somewhere deep within the castle, but thin, powerful beams of green light were also ripping into the throng of the attackers, apparently searing their flesh. Anguished screams erupted from the killendrills as smoke rose into the night air and reflected off of the afterlight of the magical flash. It was the last of the attack. One of them roared a guttural phrase, and they turned as one and half ran, half rolled down the hill, away from the castle. The main door flew open, and thirty or so horsemen burst onto the steps and rode down to the outside grass. Yelling, they pursued the beasts deep into the forest.

"I sighed and sat down on top of the stable. It was moments later that Sheenoshta found me.

"'So there you are!' he called up heartily to me from the ground in front of the stable. 'I thought those were your arrows.' I could see that he was smiling. 'You do have good eyes. The stories were correct. If I'm not wrong, I didn't count a miss among them.' He turned to look at the bodies behind him. 'Those...' he took time to count—'eight there are yours, yes?'

"'Nine,' I said.

"He seemed confused. I pointed to a killendrill near a tree that he had not counted. One of my arrows rose out of its head.

"He looked back up at me and flashed another smile. 'Best take your arrows back with you. We don't want any evidence that you were here. You've never fought killendrills before, have you?' he continued. 'Were you afraid?'

"I used my bow as a crutch to push myself up to a standing position. 'I was not. These creatures were slow and dim-witted. It was almost too easy,' I lied. 'Besides, I had an entire arsenal of archers and wizards as backup. I was merely a distraction.' I gave him a knowing look. 'Isn't that true?'

"Sheenoshta looked at the dead killendrill lying closest to the stable. 'You distracted them, all right. You distracted them to death!' He turned and smiled again. 'May I help you down?'

"I crouched and jumped to the grass, landing on my feet. 'No thank you.' I brushed myself off. 'I can manage.' I walked toward him. The way he looked at me, I could tell that I had impressed him. Perhaps he had never seen a woman handle herself in that way. 'When can we transfer the package?'

"He came closer to me. 'Now is as good a time as ever. What with the excitement of the attack and its aftermath, they'll all be too busy to be watching for spies.'

"He reached under his cloak and handed me the black-wrapped box. I looked at it in my hand, felt its weight, bounced it up and down two or three times, and smiled. 'You have no idea how this will help. The reign of the Abathet family is close to an end now. It's only a matter of time. But why fight off the killendrills?' I asked. 'Seems to me you'd want them to take down the dynasty.'

"'It's complicated,' he answered. 'There are still many of us in command who need to continue our ruse of fighting for the Abathet family. Besides,' he said, smiling, 'who wants to go from a monarchy straight into a realm overrun with killendrills? No, we need to stay in place just a bit longer. I don't want to win a battle. I want to win the war.'

"'I understand,' I answered. 'These creatures don't look like they'd be able to set up much of a decent democracy anyway.'

"He escorted me back to the portal," Kaal Bood sighed. A moth flitted back and forth over her face, threatening to land. "That was our first meeting. We met often after that, not always on military business, sometimes for pleasure. We saw each other for a little over a year." She turned her head and looked at her daughter. "And it was soon after that that I had you."

There was a silence between them. Cathyn patted her mother's stomach. "Did he ever...see me?" she asked.

Her mother smiled. "No, he never lived to see you. They discovered that he was spying for us. He was executed three days before you were born. We tried to set up a rescue mission, but we couldn't get to him in time." Her smiled faded.

Cathyn spoke through closed eyes. "So...part of the old stories were true—he was a warrior who died in battle," she yawned. Her voice was beginning to trail off into sleep.

"Yes, he was a great warrior, and he did die in the service of what is good and what is right. That is all that can be asked of a soldier." Kaal Bood patted the top of Cathyn's hand. "I always regretted that I had nothing of his to give to you as evidence of his love. But now it looks like he gave you the best part of himself."

But Cathyn was asleep. Kaal Bood could hear the gentle crackle and hum of the lightning men as they watched nearby.

CHAPTER 21
A BROKEN SPELL

When Cathyn awoke the next morning, her mother already had the fire started and was reheating some of the root tea that they had drunk the night before. The sun was bright and high in the sky already. Not noon, but not first light, either. She had slept a long time.

Cathyn forced herself up and stretched. She wanted to start the hike up the mountain right away.

"Kettle, Gamliggy, Pitts, can you walk over toward me?" she yelled into the air.

Three transparent forms moved toward her from the trees. They shimmered with the ocean now behind them, undulating slightly, as if caught in a prism.

"Let's join hands in a circle," she continued.

They did as instructed. The crackling sparked and stopped instantly as the prospectors assumed human shape.

"Top of the mornin' to you, missy!" Kettle called out.

But Cathyn was breathing hard, trying to build up power, and remain focused. "I want the three of you to concentrate on your own individual energy. If this goes as planned, we'll create a circuit that will move from person to person. I want whoever's on my left to try to energize back into your lightning form even though you're solid and you're touching me. And then I want you to send your energy over to the person on your left. That person will need to do the same the instant that he receives the energy flow from his friend."

The three men looked from one to the other and back to Cathyn again.

"Beggin' your pardon, missy," Kettle began, "but does you knows what you're doin'?"

"Yes," she answered. "I think," she added. "It's hard to explain, but I think Gamliggy was right."

The thin lightning man looked astonished.

"Does you hear that, Kettle?" Gamliggy whispered in solemn tones. "I was right." Pause. "What was I right about, mum?"

"I think it does have to do with what you talked about before, Gamliggy...that...relativity thing. It's science. It's how...energy works."

Gamliggy smiled and nodded. "I thought so. It did seem to make sense-like to me. Didn't it seem to make sense-like to yous, Pitts?"

Kettle sighed.

"It's also a kind of…faith, Kettle." She paused and smiled at the burly man. "You do trust me, don't you?" she asked.

Pitts and Gamliggy nodded their heads, eyes wide as saucers. Kettle voiced their answer. "Aye. That we do, missy. You've took us right out of the forest and out of that dark castle"—he nodded over his head—"and you brung us here. We're with you."

"Okay, then. Remember, concentrate on sending your own energy over to the person on your left." She held out her hands. "Kettle here on my left. Then Gamliggy holding his hand and facing me. Then Pitts holding my hand." She waited until the group was in position. "On the count of three, now. Ready? One… two…three!"

Kaal Bood had stopped stirring the tea and now stood up to watch the curious circle.

Kettle was the first to spark back to vibrational life. His body glowed wildly, like a living fireball, a much higher energy arc than any of them had ever seen before. It was the first time that any of the prospectors had ever been able to return to energy form while holding on to a living thing. The energy "flame" flashed out on Kettle and then flashed back onto Gamliggy. Gamliggy held that state for ten heartbeats, flashed off, and seemed to send the energy "flame" over to Pitts, who held it for half that length of time. When it flashed out on him, it flashed back on again, this time onto Cathyn. Cathyn had become a lightning being, just like the three prospectors.

Kaal Bood looked hard at her daughter. She did not notice any undue stress as the energy field, now whiter and more intense than the other three, pulsed from her body. Cathyn's eyes were closed in concentration, but there was no look of fear or pain on her face, just a kind of quiet and severe study. She seemed to be in total control.

The energy "flame" flashed out on Cathyn and moved again over to Kettle. The circuit continued on like this more times than she could count, flashing on and off quicker with each new "owner." It looked to Kaal Bood as if a train made of light was moving in a circle, building up speed as it went, until finally it seemed as though the entire circle was lit up as one complete column of unbroken light. It gave the impression of a swirling, phosphorescent whirlpool. Just looking at it made Kaal Bood feel dizzy, off-balance. Like she was moving. The sand around the circle group was beginning to kick up wisps of clouds, causing small tornado-like apparitions to form. Small trinkets of crystal flew from the tornado as the sand was energized into glass. And then with a loud pop, a final plume of pure energy shot out in a straight line from the top of Cathyn's body, right up into the sky above them. Kaal Bood looked up, but could not see where it ended. A line of flickering light made a straight path up and continued on, uninterrupted, into the sky. Within a moment, the "flame" flashed out and was gone completely. Except for the lapping of the nearby ocean waves, all was quiet.

The four continued holding hands, afraid to drop them and disconnect. Cathyn was the first one to break the circuit. She let go of the two prospectors' hands and opened her eyes. She held both of her own hands up as if to illustrate her success.

Kettle was still holding on to Gamliggy, who was still holding on to Pitts, but there was no longer any normal solid contact with Cathyn. They remained wholly human. They dared not breathe, only using enough movement to look at one another with wonder in their eyes. Slowly, very slowly, they dropped their hands and disconnected from one another. They were still solid men.

"Whoooooweee!" Kettle screamed. "Missy, you done it! You broke the spell!"

Gamliggy looked at his hands, smiled, and walked over to Kettle and patted him on the back. "Does you feels that, Kettle?" he asked. "That's me a-pattin' you on the back all by meself!"

Pitts merely stood still, looking at his hands and crying, tears running down his cheeks. A few hairs from his ponytail had become dislodged during the ordeal and now hung in his face.

Kettle and Gamliggy were forced to sidle up to him to give him comfort, putting their hands on his shoulders and saying things like, "There, there, Pitts. It's all right. We're all right now. Missy's gone and fixed us up right good."

"I knows she has," he sniffed. He was crying and smiling at the same time. "I knows she has. I never had any doubts about her. I knew she was the real thing when first I seen her."

Kettle moved away from his two friends and stood in front of Cathyn. "We can'ts thank you enough, missy. You done us proud. If it weren't destiny that we met you, then I don't know what is." He extended his hand out to her.

She looked at his outstretched hand, gave him a curious smile, and grabbed him around the neck instead in a strong hug. "You three saved our lives," she whispered into his ear. "Don't you ever forget that. We would be dead if you hadn't shown up." She let go of Kettle and looked at his face. Tears had welled up in his eyes. He just stood there nodding.

"We're forever indebted to you, mum," Gamliggy called out, patting Pitts's hand in between his own two, Pitts still crying big tears of joy.

Kaal Bood walked over to her daughter and put her hand on her shoulder. "I'm so very proud of you, my darling," she said. "Seems like you're every bit the sorcerer your father was."

Cathyn looked at her mother. "He would be proud of you as well." Cathyn smiled. Now it was her eyes that filled up.

Pausing, the mother warrior turned to the now all-human prospectors.

"Gentlemen!" she called out. "Shall we climb?"

"Lead the way, mum," answered Kettle. "We'll take the rear."

It took most of the day to make it up the mountain and work their way back to the woods at the top. This time, Cathyn led Tempest up the steep path without a rider. The only obstacles in their paths were an occasional reptile or mountain creature and a few loose rocks that sent Gamliggy tumbling down to the previous landing. He actually laughed when he had finished rolling and sat up.

"Look at this!" he yelled from below the others. "I gots meself all scraped up!"

"Welcome to the solid world!" Cathyn yelled back.

"Good things you landed on your bum!" Kettle added as he and Pitts stumbled back down to help him resume their climb.

By the time they came to the summit, both Cathyn and her mother had gotten on Tempest for their final journey through Abathet Woods, Kaal Bood in the front of the saddle, Cathyn in the back. Their way back through the woods was uneventful. The three former lightning men would point out various spots where they had set up camp during certain seasons or a particular area where they had panned for lightning gems. Kettle found the place where they had met Lady Abathet and Captain Melog for the first time. Gamliggy found his favorite lookout tree. The prospectors seemed to enjoy being tour guides for their new friends. It had been their home for such a long time, there was almost an unspoken sadness to leave it behind for good.

Finally, they reached the end of Abathet Woods, and the true beginning of their return home. They all silently moved through the curved opening of thick trees and out onto the pathway. Dusk was approaching.

Kaal Bood turned in the saddle and addressed the three prospectors, looking down at them from her horse. "Well, this is where we say our good-byes. What will you three do now? Where will you go?"

Kettle spoke up. "Well, ma'am, we all three comes from the same village just two days' hike from here. We'll return home and start up life again."

"We'll be livin'!" Pitts called out. His joy was almost tangible.

"Will you continue prospecting?" Cathyn asked.

"Oh, I thinks we're done with the prospectin' life," Gamliggy answered. "No more lightning gems for these lucky blokes."

Kaal Bood looked hard at the three men. "If we ever cross over here again, can we call on you?"

"Without a moment's hesitation, Commander," Kettle replied. "Mognast's Clearing is where we live." He pointed down another side of the mountain. "Right down there. Straight on till you come to the first village."

"And you'll be welcomed over to our side as well," Kaal Bood added. "We live in Normaneys. If the way is ever opened permanently, you make your ways there and ask for us. Eventually..."—she paused— "eventually, maybe our two sides will be able to live together and trade ideas and materials to make both of our worlds better. That was one of our goals, after all."

"Perhaps you're right, mum," Kettle agreed.

It was after they stood near the horse and his riders, sharing the last pieces of meat and fruit from the morning meal and talking quietly, that the three former prospectors and the two warriors parted company. One more series of hand-holdings and hand-pattings, and then Cathyn watched the men walk down their side of the mountain and disappear over the edge, all three waving their arms, but looking straight ahead toward their destination. The warrior and her daughter turned Tempest silently and rode on.

Nighttime was now approaching. It didn't take long for Cathyn to notice a change in their surroundings. She looked at the darkening sky and realized that she once again recognized some of the constellations sharpening into focus before her. Some of those stars were old friends. And some of them were new friends. And some of them had already turned, but it all made each pattern in the night sky look better for it. The air was becoming cooler. She could see the breath from her mouth misting in front of her. She could almost smell the fires from their neighbors' chimneys. Tempest was moving faster now, blowing wisps of vapor in the air as he moved. He was on familiar ground now. A few scattered snowflakes began to appear in the cold, dark air around them, and Cathyn knew that her mother had found the path and that they were on their way back home.

ABOUT THE AUTHOR

David Newhouse is a teacher who lives with his family in Maryland. He is also one of the founding members of the long-standing jazz / progrock band, The Muffins. Contact him at:

ndnewhouse@comast.net
www.ndavidnewhouse.com